Tango Fandango

G.B. LAMB

To order additional copies of this book, contact:
Bookwhip
1-855-339-3589
https://www.bookwhip.com

Credits and Thanks...

To my son Bill Brendle for composing and orchestrating "Tango Fandango". Its lush melody is a perfect embodiment of the music that inspires and compels the drama of the dance. Bill is well known in the Latin and Brazilian music scene, having been musically associated with Sergio Mendez and his own group, Sambaguru for many years. Recently, Bill did the orchestrations for "Summer", the 2017 award winning musical currently playing on Broadway. "Tango Fandango" is available on his website: www.bbrendle.com.

To my longtime friend Susie Lewis for her skillful proofreading and encouragement during the final manuscript production process.

To Israel Vela, the dashing tanguero on the cover, who so gallantly partnered me for the tango competitions and shows we were lucky enough to participate in.

Finally, thank you to my fellow California tango afficionados whom I laughed and cried with, and the many lessons they taught me in pursuit of the perfect tango.

GRACIAS A TODAS Y VIVA EL TANGO!

La Salida

(The Departure)

As the music beckons, the tango dancers enter the dance floor two by two; willing players in a unique performance. The men bravely face the women; the women in turn appear flushed, expectant, and ready to follow where led. After a brief moment of mutual acknowledgement, they take their positions as the music begins. Taking two steps forward, the man advances into the woman's space, requiring her retreat. They pause briefly. Subtly but bravely, he continues his advance, pressing on, intent on his mission, mentally strategizing his next move. Formulating his plan silently, he maneuvers the woman into a side step. She complies and they complete their Salida—their feet together, toes touching toes—their bodies touching heart to heart. A hesitation—a breath—a gathering of forces, and off they go, abandoning themselves to the dance, their heartbeats in synch; the music intoxicating them like a tropical cocktail.

Prologue

Yucatan Peninsula: Spring of 1980

My name is Marie Jordan, and I have an addiction. I feed it regularly and passionately, which brought me to this place near the sunny meridian of the world during the not so sunny meridian of my life.

I'd heard that dancing the tango is a journey of the soul that's led by the heart. But, not just any tango . . . the Argentine tango. If that were even remotely true, I wanted to take that journey. I knew I had to find out . . . to depart from my life of mediocrity. I guess, in truth, I came here in order to escape from myself. But as most journeys begin with an impetus borne of a need or desire which leads one to a destination suitable to the fulfilling of that need, mine was no different. So to make sense of it all, I'll take a minute or two to begin at the beginning.

I had a need alright. Six months into widowhood, I was feeling alone and bored. I tried tennis . . . too tough on the joints. Bowling gave me a headache (too much noise); ballroom dancing was pretty expensive, although I did meet some interesting mature men (mature in age only as it turned out). Scuba diving nearly drowned me, and square dancing . . . well, those skirts . . . forget it. "Try the tango", my adventurous friend, Dixie, suggested. A chorus of agreement arose from my well-meaning friends. "It's so romantic, and besides, we can go to the dances together. You wanted something different. Come on!" I was curious, but apprehensive, having seen the flashy footwork and four-inch spiked heels worn by the glamorous and exotic *tangueras* I had seen in a show from Buenos Aires that came to L.A. My enthusiastic buddies had taken up the dance right after that show, and couldn't stop talking about how "erotic" it was, and how I would love it, and how many great guys I would meet at the parties. Right. Then, as fate would have it, I received an ad in the mail, for a class being held at the studio they were attending, with an attractive discount if I would "take a chance and experience the intrigue of the Argentine tango in ten easy lessons". Normally skeptical, and with some misgivings, I nonetheless paid the fee (always up for a bargain), took the classes, enjoyed myself immensely and must admit to having mastered the dance with a modicum of style. As an added bonus, I found my classmates to be a fascinating and lively lot. Doctors, psychologists, teachers, and several ardent "lotharios" danced with me as the instructor announced after each new step was taught; "change partners, please". We concentrated earnestly, gradually learning the intricate floor patterns, and trying at the same time to embody the "tango attitude" we had seen displayed on T.V. and the stage shows. I did fine, and even enjoyed the process. I was feeling accomplished and exhilarated at my progress, and even a bit cocky, until I discovered how wrong I was, as my first humbling experience thrust itself upon me at our "tango initiation" in an out of town tango club.

So, now I'm getting dressed for a "*milonga*". It's a dance, not a drink, and it's a dance party. I decide to wear my red chiffon with the tight bodice, un-box my red silk dance shoes, and proceed with the underpinnings. On go the bra, and the matching red panties, the sheerest of stockings and then the dress. Oops . . . too tight . . . damn! Off it comes, and the bra, and the panties. What am I thinking? It's just a dance—maybe it'll help me lose weight. I settled for a basic black number, plus accessories, twisted my hair into a sophisticated bun, and added a flirtatious red flower, just for effect.

As my ardent friends and I arrived at the dance on that fateful October night, a group of guys were just ahead of us, making the evening promising. I paid at the door, had my hand stamped with the outline of some strange red animal, and entered a dimly lit room. I strained my eyes, adjusting to the candlelit interior, trying to spot my friends at one of the tables surrounding an impossibly small parquet dance floor. I stood mesmerized as the dancing couples passed by, totally oblivious to me, seemingly lost to the deft maneuverings of a sensuous choreography. It seemed as if the dance took them away, setting them apart from the rest of us, to a destination known only to them. One look and I was hooked. I didn't know why, but at least I knew. I wanted—"that"—whatever "that" was. Of course, I knew it was all an illusion. Supreme efforts look effortless, seemingly devoted couples part hastily when the music ends, and trusted alliances are breached all the time. At the start of each musical overture the curtain rises, there are new players, and it all begins again. Nevertheless . . . even for a three minute thrill . . . I wanted—"that".

I'm not considered beautiful, but at the least I've been told I'm attractive. I waited expectantly through a number of dances, while several men promisingly looked my way, but as I made a responsive move toward them, a girl to my left or right or from behind strode past me to their welcoming arms. I sat down again. What was wrong? What am I missing? Finally spotting Dixie, I joined her at the table, and humbled myself to ask her to enlighten me. "What is going on with these guys? I want to dance, and nobody's asking me. How do these other women know they want them?" She smiled Dixie style and told me to watch closely and she would teach me about "the come-on".

It took me a bit to catch on, but soon, I observed the barely perceptible nod that a man would send in the direction of a woman to signal her to come and dance with him. Why don't they just ask, I wondered. But, I gamely waited, and watched, and waited. Aha! I think I've been nodded at, finally. As fate would have it, my one and only tango dance that night was with a dear fellow, who could barely cross the floor. I think he was on the other side of ninety, and seemingly near death. As I came to him with trepidation, all I could think of was what I would do if he should keel mid-tango, pinning me beneath him like an old man during a sexual liason in a seedy motel room. But, a tango is a tango, and as I approached, he gamely drew himself up to a respectable imitation of a dashing latin. Well, as it turns out, he thought he was God's gift to the tango, and to beat all, he wasn't very patient, either. No subtlety there about his displeasure as I stumbled and tripped all over him, every lesson of mine forgotten. I felt clumsy and inept and had no idea what he expected me to do as he stood expectantly, posing in tango attitude, waiting for me to perform some balance-defying move that escaped me. He grimaced as I almost took out his manly pride with a poorly-placed flick of my foot. (I never could master the *"gancho"* maneuver). As soon as the music ended, he mutated back to a doddery old fellow, barely able to guide me back to my waiting cohorts who exhibited much restraint after watching the comedy I had provided them. I spent the rest of the evening humbled by the experience, but determined to rise to the challenge. I would show everybody. I would become the greatest tango dancer in our time. Or, at least in Southern California. How hard could it be?

The tango muse smiled upon me when the opportunity presented itself in the mail the very next day in the form of a beautifully colored brochure:

TANGO IN THE TROPICS!
Attention tango lovers!
Join us in the romantic tropics of the Yucatan
for a fantastic three day tango workshop!
Classes taught by some of the foremost teachers in the world!
You'll learn everything you've wanted to know about the tango and more!
AUGUST 16, 17,18
Five-star hotel—Meals included
Live music in a romantic setting
"NO PARTNER NEEDED"
Contact Senor Efren Montoya for registration and payment information.

Well now, that was a sign! I had run into the dashing but arrogant Señor Montoya at an earlier class in L.A. Think of that - he's the official tango workshop contact person! A three days in the tropics workshop! He had told me he was an engineer. Of course, he didn't give me a tumble at the time, but then, things could change, couldn't they?

It was easy to muster an enthusiastic assent for a weekend tango tryst from Dixie and then we pounced on our third musketeer, Dawn, persuading her to join us. Thus our merry band of three eagerly completed our forms, filled in all the required personal data, and sent them off to the promoters (along with a hefty deposit) the very next day. We were sure it would be worth it.

Thus, my intimacy with the tango was to begin. It beckoned and I answered the call, setting out on an exotic terpsichorean pilgrimage to the eastern shores of the Caribbean Sea—that sunny, steamy, sensuous clime where, for three nights and four days, my fellow devotees and I would live in that boundary world of nocturnal mysteries. What were we looking for? Would we find it? Had we known the answers to those questions beforehand, we all might have stayed safely at home. But nothing at home would have given us the adventure of our lives.

Figure One

EL MOLINETE
(The Wheel)

Picture a man and a woman on a dance floor: the lights are dim and they face each other resolutely, challenging each other with their eyes and their manner. The man holds the woman at the extremity of his outstretched arms and begins to spin, using one foot to propel the other, establishing an axis. The woman is his co-conspirator in this circular duet. With her body facing his, she moves swiftly around him, creating momentum as her feet deftly trace the circumference of their private arena. In the analogy of the bullfight, he wields the cape, and she is the bull. He initiates the circle, leading her around as if to display his control of the relationship. But he cannot turn without her compliance. So—who is leading whom?

The room was set up in typical tango club fashion. Small round tables were circled around the dance floor, topped with white linen cloths, a flickering candle and a small vase of fresh flowers for this special occasion. There was a line of chairs along the wall, for the folks who just wanted to watch, or had no partners. The dreaded wall. Would I spend most of my time there like a wilted flower waiting to be picked? I'm not considered beautiful, but it seemed to me I was attractive enough to not have to sit in a chair on the wall. Well, time would tell.

It was our first dance party, the kick-off to our long awaited tango pilgrimage. Ah yes, ten-hours of classes, food, classes, food, and a nightly *milonga* (with food) where we could wear our sexy, exotic and expensive apparel which, after all the food, would barely fit us by the last day. My amigos, Dixie and Dawn and myself (they called us the three butterflies) had survived our first day, soaked our tired tootsies, and came eagerly tonight, for a chance to practice what we'd learned.

Dixie and Dawn were already on the floor dancing, and I sat watching my fellow classmates, determined not to feel sorry for myself. I would amuse myself by observing the fascinating behavior of the crowd. After only one day of classes, the wheel of romance among us emotionally charged creatures had begun to turn. Here I was, lustily longing for Ricardo, who cared nothing for me, but apparently pined after my little blonde friend, Dixie, who had an eye for Eduardo who was obsessed with me. Then there was Carlos, who chased us all in search of something inside himself he could not define. Perhaps he was longing for an identity he hoped the tango would birth in him. Yes, the whole scene turned and turned, round and round it went, like a dog chasing its tail . . . a wheel of passion just like the *Molinete* in the tango. And when the dance is over, the players disperse, refresh, regroup and with the first strains of the whiningly seductive *bandoneon,* reassemble to create another bewitching scene . . . different music, different players, but the same ritual of love and expectancy.

As I sat mesmerized, it seemed as though one dance ran into the next, a never ending, provocative scenario. It occurred to me that after only one day of classes, people began to reveal a lot about themselves. For instance, some men didn't like the responsibility of leading, like Carlos. Some of the women were not comfortable with the loss of control and didn't like to follow. Elena came to mind, as she had just taken the empty seat beside me. Then, there were the totally dedicated—the tango aficionados. These true *milongeros,* married or not, were rarely sitting, preferring to dance the night away. Their understanding wives shared their love for the dance as well as their men for others to dance with. I loved these men, and I loved dancing with them. They each gave their own message during the dance. In Eduardo's arms, I felt safe, but a little uneasy, not sure I could match his intensity. In Ricardo's arms, I felt controlled but oh, so passionate. Of course, then there were the hesitant, unsure ones like Carlos in whose arms I felt . . . nothing. Oh, well!

So now, here I was, sitting on a chair along the wall at a *milonga*. Oh, how I hated sitting on these chairs. However, I held my disdain and chatted amicably with my equally anticipatory new-found chums, waiting impatiently for someone to bring me to my feet to dance (please, God!). I tried to spot Dixie or Dawn, but they were still dancing somewhere in the darkness when out of the corner of my eye I spotted Carlos, his short and wiry frame advancing eagerly in my direction. As he approached, I began rising to meet him when he turned to my left and hesitantly reached for Elena's hand. Rats!

Being afflicted with a sometimes annoying dose of optimism, I chose to ignore my rising impatience, and used this "downtime" to contemplate. I'd heard that dancing the tango is the purest form of communication between a man and a woman. Inspired by the plaintive music and soulful verse that he hears, each dance is choreographed on the spot by the man; his body leading the woman's, heart to heart and soul to soul. In the true Argentine tango, so we were taught in class this morning, the heart is where the steps pass through on their way from the head to the feet. In fact, while dancing in the pure tango style, the man and woman are so intimately connected that she can feel the rhythm of his beating heart and the really good women dancers can respond to him with beautifully executed steps. This, of course, being enhanced by 5 inch heels and the flirty skirt of a carefully chosen dress.

Oh how I longed to dance like that . . . to look like that . . . to really feel totally involved with another human's thoughts, all the way to the core of his being. It seemed to me a perfect fusion between two people; seamless, with no differentiation between where the man ends and the woman begins . . . one in thought and motion. Yet I knew that such a surrender would likely take its toll.

Yet, I was willing to chance it. But why? Why did it have a such a mysterious hold on me? Why does my heart leap so when I hear the music? How can I mitigate the feeling of loss when at the end of the dance my partner leaves to find another? Is it because during the moments of the dance the experience is so beautiful—so penetrating—that it's worth the loss? Or, is it because I know this experience will be repeated with my next partner? And the next. That is if I ever get a partner. Uh oh. There I go again.

And then, my contemplations were interrupted when glancing up, I saw Ricardo sauntering my way. I noticed him in my first class; debonair and sure of himself. He was tall, of an angular frame. He was all at once graceful and ungainly—handsome and yet not so handsome. He had a boyish twinkle in his eyes, and when he smiled, crinkles appeared at the corners of his eyes which belied his otherwise youthful face. His smile . . . well, it captivated me. It was broad and kind, revealing large white rows of teeth, slightly gapped in the center and sitting evenly in his square jaw. His voice, though, was the essence of his persona—it tumbled out of his mouth and fell like rolling stones on the ears of his listeners. It was an announcing voice—clear, distinct and important. Oh, how I wanted to dance with him! As he came towards me, I began to rise, and barely caught myself as he beckoned to Sally, sitting demurely beside me. How nervy, I screamed inside. Passing me up like that. Doesn't he know how great I am to dance with? In five minutes, I'm going back to the hotel. And then, I spotted him coming through the door . . . Efren.

It was soon after my escape into those first tango classes—an escape from the laborious chastity of womanhood—that I met Efren. Fragile and overly sentimental I was, raw and vulnerable from the dreadful fact of losing Jerry, my first love, adoring husband, best and closest friend. As mature and "over it" as I tried to be, eagerly open to all the newly found friendships and the erstwhile dancing partners I was beginning to meet, I really wasn't ready for Efren. He had asked me to dance on that fateful night, and I did so, quite well, as a matter of fact. I was enthralled with his poetic soulful manner and craggy, brooding face. His slightly sagging jowls promised with advancing age to develop a profusion of velvety folds, reminding me of a beguiling little Sharpei pup. The corners of his mouth rested seriously, rising only at an amusing story, or to greet a friend. Yet, it was a handsome face, full of manliness and pride, its somber expression softened by sensitive brown eyes, flecked with grey. He stood solid—wide at the shoulder and slim at the waist, and I guessed him to be fortyish; close to my age. He danced beautifully, with a natural flair and feel for the music, and he held me with a shuddering passion as we danced, encircling me with his essence, inviting me to know the deepest part of himself. Why did he hold me so? It both startled and beguiled me. How was I supposed to react? Should I ignore it and say nothing, or respond, be receptive and run the risk of being perceived as presumptuous. I did the only thing I could do under the circumstances. I fell for him like a fool under a spell. Naturally, it put me at a great disadvantage with this proud and confident man, and he immediately sensed my weakness for him. After that night, when we were at the same dances, he passed me by several times before asking me to dance, and when he did dance with me, it was usually in class, taking me to him and holding me with as much passion as I could bear. It was as though he held the key to my locked up cache of love feelings, the ones I had smothered and buried away for the two years since Jerry died.

Those burning-in-the-pit-of-my stomach-feelings. That sunburst of sensation beginning down there, deep inside, just below the spot where hunger begins, and radiating upward until it set fire to my heart. The tango allowed him to use the key to the cache, but when my feelings were released and revealed themselves to him, he ducked back into his own little niche and locked himself safely inside, leaving me out. It was horrible and cold out there, and yet it felt so good to be held closely again in a man's arms, I relished the experience. I luxuriated in the smell of his cologne on my clothes long after we parted. Yes, I was hooked, and wasted the rest of the evening pining away, waiting for him to ask me to dance again, which he never did. I dreamt about him that night, and many other nights after that. I had planned to be a dilettante and slip away, untouched, but it was too late.

And now, there he was. Efren. As he entered the room, advancing forward in his suave manner, he affably greeted those he knew until those grey-brown eyes became locked with mine. My heart beating wildly, I smiled as coolly and demurely as possible, saying "Efren; how nice to see you." All the while, heated flashes began coursing upward through my body, coming to rest, I was sure, on my burning cheeks. My mind was working furiously on what would happen next when he said, "It's good to see you looking so well—will you do me the honor?", and extended his hand, inviting me to dance.

We danced warmly and well, and he held me tenderly this time, like a cherished treasure. I hoped he wouldn't notice the tremble of my hand or feel the beating of my heart as I leaned into him with my new-found mastery of the tango position. How incredibly sweet it was to be in his arms again. As he released his hold on me to lead me around himself in a *Molinete*, I caught the pungent scent of his cologne, bringing back a flood of memories and all too familiar feelings. He turned me this way and that, and caught me up in a tight hold while setting me on one foot, causing me to nearly lose my balance. Damn! I looked up questioningly into his eyes. An apology was in his returning glance, but there was something else in the depths of his pupils which I could not decipher. What was he thinking? Oh, but I didn't want to be a fool again. Yet the feelings I got from him were so exquisitely poignant, I wanted them to last forever. Before I could sort it all out, the dance was over, and then, amazingly, he asked for another. Now what? These Argentine men, I thought. Go figure. A few minutes ago, I was sitting along the wall, feeling sorry for myself, and now, I was dancing with Efren—not once, but twice! And this was a waltz; of all the dances, my least favorite. I never seemed to get the rhythm right. But before I could dwell on my insecurities, I was being swept along by his long strides, turning and swirling with his chin resting on the top of my head.

As we waltzed around the room, I could see the other girls sitting on the chairs along the wall, where I was just moments ago, watching us intently. The very thought that they might be envious of me buoyed my spirits, and I held my body more elegantly, growing at least an inch taller with the effort so that my forehead now touched his chin, and I could feel the stubble of his beard against my moist skin. Lovely! I knew that this was the best waltz I had ever waltzed, and as the final chords brought us to the *cadenzia*, I felt quite smug. Out of the corner of my eye, I saw two of the girls from the chairs approaching us, probably to snatch him away before the next selection began. Just then, Efren walked us toward a less crowded area of the floor. In my mind's eye, I could picture the expression on the faces of my classmates, now thwarted in their attempts to dance with him. I confess that I had an untoward feeling of superiority at the prospect.

As we strode away, I turned to give them an apologetic glance. There was always a shortage of men, it seemed, and the women became very competitive. I was on the other end of the dilemma many times. Feeling a bit sympathetic, I resolved to explain to them later that Efren was an old friend whom I had not seen for over a year, and that we had a lot of catching up to do. I didn't want any hard feelings, but at this point, Efren seemed to enjoy my dancing, and if he was asking, I was dancing. And then, the small orchestra began the beautiful *"Tango Fandango"*. I knew it was Efren's favorite. He once again extended his hand, and without a word, brought me to dance position, nestling me once more in his arms. And then, it hit me. There appeared to be a change in the relationship between Efren and myself. His guard was down. The wheel had turned. He was pursuing *me*; asking me without words for some sort of validation. I could tell in his manner—in the way he began this dance. As we took the first steps of the *Salida*, his embrace was softer, and less demanding. He waited longer for me to complete my footwork, giving me a chance to practice some newly learned embellishments. I began to experiment with the steps, being careful to remain in his lead—not wanting to break the spell. I glanced up at him when I had a chance, and he seemed lost in thought, a million miles away. Oh, how I wanted to say something, ask questions, comfort him and love him. But I would not make the same mistake again.

We finished our dance and exchanged smiles. After thanking him, and before he could speak and shatter my thin veneer of confidence, I turned quickly to go. Knowing his eyes were following me, hips swaying provocatively, I swept through the swinging doors and headed out.

*   *   *

Figure Two

EL ESPEJO
(The Mirror—Reflections on a Tango)

When I dance with a man, I mirror his lead; his right foot moves forward and causes my left foot to move backward. His left hand holds my right hand. He turns me and we are in a promenade, facing a new direction together. His right foot is against my left foot, the sides touching. El Espejo. I am a perfect image of him—I mirror his intentions. But dancing the tango goes deeper still, as I am also compelled to mirror his feelings . . . his soul for the dance. I can feel his intensity, or the lack of it. I respond accordingly. Does he mirror my thoughts also? I am in his world, but is he in mine?

As he maneuvered her around the impossibly small dance floor, Efren Jesus Montoya held his partner in an enveloping, intimate embrace. As soon as his arms went around a woman like this, he could not escape the need to tighten them and draw her close. He liked the feeling of offering a haven to his partner, a sense of security, and a shelter from the outside energies of the other tango students who surrounded them on the dance floor. Here, in this exotic location, far from his home in Argentina, he was finally beginning to feel like his old self. Tanned by the peninsular sun and relaxed for the first time in many months, he could feel himself wanting to let down the barriers that dominated the relationships in his old life. It was his time to assess and evaluate his existence.

It was the first night of "Tango in the Tropics", and as many of the dancers did, he sacrificed at the altar of the tango the burden of his hurts and disappointments, and they always drifted away as he danced. It had the effect of clearing his head, and it helped him to put a different perspective on his thoughts. If only he could just keep dancing like this without having to interact with his partner. He wanted no words from her, just silence and a good tango. It wasn't as though he didn't enjoy talking to this American woman. In fact, he had danced with her before at a tango club in Los Angeles a couple of years ago. As he held her and felt the gentle curve of her waist beneath his hand, memories began flooding back, and he just wanted to think, without interruption. Why? Was it the music? It was slow and plaintive; a song of a man's search for love through the eyes of a troubadour. Efren was on that search, and as he moved through the dance, his mind moved back through time. He began to sort things out in his mind . . . to think back . . . to unroll the past like a ribbon and pull it across his mind and out of his heart where it had bound him up for so long. His thoughts rushed back to that day—a day that comes to each of us sooner or later, when we know that life from that moment on will be different forever.

While the music carried his feet along, Efren allowed his mind to take him back eight years, pacing at the foot of his mother Irena's bed. In all of his 28 years, he had never had so much fear, although he had been at his mother's bedside before—in fact, several times before. One of the most frightening times was the June after his graduation ceremony from the upper form school. His Auntie Mae had grudgingly decided to attend. Grudgingly because her own son—her only son (outranked in seniority by two dreadfully domineering sisters) had flunked out of that same school barely two years before. This particularly rankled his Auntie, as she, the oldest sister of Efren's mother, made a lifetime career of lording her superiority over the more beautiful Irena. Especially because of the lifestyle her marriage afforded. Indeed, compared to his Auntie, Efren and his family, though they lived decently, lived moderately.

Although graduation day had begun optimistically for his mother, it soon deteriorated as it always did as the day wore on, and she began complaining to his father of her imagined snubbing from her sister. His father argued with Irena, taking Mae's side as he always did, and then left for the Tango Club which further angered his mother. This scene ended as it always did with the responsibility of placating his mother left to Efren. Irena had perfected this whole scenario as well as her resulting illness, and she heaped praises on Efren for his ministrations to her. However, if he denied her the attention she sought, she manipulated and deflated his ego by bringing him down with denigrating statements such as; "You don't have time for your Mother, eh? Well, you think you're so smart, but you'll get your comeuppance one day, young man. Just you wait!" These manipulations created in him a desperate need for his mother's approval, and gave her the satisfaction of keeping at least one of the two men in the household under her control at all times. It created a situation of such extraordinary disparity and co-dependence, that Efren very nearly had a serious nervous breakdown in his adolescent years.

It could be said that Efren's salvation came from his concerned older and more experienced cousin, who shared with him several female courtesans whose erotic and tender ministering became an intoxicating elixir to him. It was quite a revelation to Efren, who, after his first furtive liaison, was bound to the sensations and satisfactions he derived from exercising his natural prowess in the game of love and the mysterious ways of a man with a woman. He was happy to pay for their favors as none demanded his faithfulness or emotional involvement, only his considerable virility. Nor did any of these women inspire him to surrender his fragile ego or yield his soul, guarded as it was from true love. That is until one day, in the middle of his sophomore year at college, when he first laid eyes on Sara.

He met her on a blustery winter day, both of them seeking shelter from the howling wind in the library of the University campus. As they laughed and talked that day, he fell in love quickly and he vowed he would have her. She was a freshman; young and eager, and so bright—studying to be a psychologist. She wanted to work with children, to give them a healthy mental and emotional way out of their problems. She explained to him how she wanted to help them build their self-esteem and a sense of where they fit into life. If only he could learn that for himself, he thought. She agreed to a date that very night—the first of many—and Efren was joyously smitten. Here was a woman who knew him, understood him, and loved him tenderly. How exquisite was her mouth when her lilting voice trilled his name. "Efren, mi vida" she would say, and so often; "Oh, Efren, you are taking my breath away!" His mind drifted again to their last dance together. She danced like an angel, and nestled into him so that the top of her head lay perfectly in the curve of his neck, the blonde tendrils of her hair tickling his cheek ever so lightly. He remembered the feel of her silk dress against his hand, like her skin, soft and smooth. He could feel the warmth of her back radiating through the filmy fabric, warming his hand as he held her. Later in the evening, long after he left her, as he was walking home he could still catch the smell of her perfume dancing in and out of his consciousness with every capricious breeze. He relished the memory of the lingering scent of her on his jacket, his shirt, his chest as he undressed and readied himself for sleep. "If only . . . if only . . .", he thought, and though he knew the foolishness of it, he could not stop himself from thinking it.

Efren knew his mother suspected him of dallying with women, but before Sara, she seemed to block the thought from her mind and let him have his fun. But as his relationship with Sara blossomed, his desire to be with other women waned, and by the time he graduated, Efren and Sara were "an item". Their social circle looked on them as a couple, probably the next to marry. They looked so right together . . . Efren standing tall and dark next to her ethereal and delicate frame. They both loved to tango, and they were happy and compatible with their friends, who enjoyed being around them. In fact, Sara's only critic was Efren's mother. She could never accept Sara's Germanic ancestry, although there were countless socially acceptable Germans in Argentina. Her disdain for Sara was clear and it escalated with each visit, so that soon Efren began to realize that if it wasn't the ethnic problem, it would be something else, for his mother would never relinquish her place in his affections to another female. He felt trapped.

Yet, he tried to be there for his Mama, to be loyal and concerned. But soon, he could no longer hide from her the fact that something had changed. His visits to her room during her illnesses became less frequent. His attentiveness began to lag—he became impatient to be dismissed from hearing her litany of complaints. His darting eyes and shrugging shoulders gave away his flagging interest in her latest symptoms, and she noticed. He knew that she knew something was different. His suspicions were confirmed right after that Sunday evening when he had daringly brought Sara to supper and introduced her to the family. After a reasonably pleasant dinner, he had returned to the dining room to get Sara some coffee when he overheard his mother talking to his Auntie Mae in the kitchen. She spoke with venom about "that little German-Italian tart batting her big blue eyes at my Efren like that. Who does she think she is?" In a panic that Sara might hear, he abruptly abandoned the coffee and the family, excusing their hasty departure and getting her out of there. He never brought her back. In fact, their affair was temporarily interrupted when Irena got the bright idea of talking his father into sending Efren to California as a graduation gift. He would spend the summer with some cousins who headed up the Argentine Association in the Los Angeles area. "Have a good time before you come back, and then you can find a job," they said. And off he went. It was there that he met the American woman—the one he was dancing with now. She was small and vivacious, and as they danced, he remembered that she fell for him in a big way, and he wondered briefly how she might feel about him now.

Of course, back then in L. A., he could have cared less. Irena's strategy had worked as far as he and Sara were concerned, and as he filled his nights with countless dances and careless love, his memory of Sara became less intense, so that by the time he returned to Argentina, he was even happy to be home and back in the orbit of his mother's world; catered to and fussed over. Irena had won again, and he was hers alone. Well, almost alone. And he was almost happy. What was this hold she had over him? Why did she want to smother him so, and why did he let her? Efren knew he had to have answers, and he made a decision to have a talk with his Auntie Mae. He recalled the afternoon they sat sipping tea in the garden rotunda at his Auntie's house and the story of his Mama's life began to be told to him.

Irena and Mae grew up in a turbulent home, mostly because of their father's drinking bouts, coupled with their mother's frequent infidelities. Mores being what they were in the budding new century, these infidelities were carried out with the utmost discretion. However, even the cleverest of women such as their mother was would most certainly make a fatal error in judgment, and become grist for the gossip mill by being discovered at some rendezvous by the most garrulous of females. Human nature being what it is, the incident would be deliciously carried one to another throughout the community, until it be told to the wronged spouse, for his or her own good, of course. This resulted in many families being uprooted as either the mother or father would leave home, or the infraction would be endured and overlooked by the spouse for the sake of the marriage and the children, and the cycle would begin again. In the case of Irena and Mae, both parents were less than worthy, and the sisters stuck together, made the best of it and resolved one day to leave for good.

According to Efren's Auntie Mae, she, the eldest by five years, married first and well. She and her husband, a lawyer, produced three babies in short order, who were loved and catered to by their grandparents. In fact, the arrival of the grandchildren seemed to improve the dynamics within the family, and peace reigned for the time being. Meanwhile, Irena came of age, and having developed into a bright and beautiful young woman, (though willful), she was able to procure a job as a hostess at an upscale mountain resort on the lake at Bariloche. Her plan was to work summers as a hostess while cultivating friends and admirers among the clientele, who were the proverbial rich and famous of Argentina. Realizing her need for becoming educated and cultured, her Mama contacted a distant cousin, Sophia, who lived in a town which was near a small but well accredited college. Through persistence and determination, Irena was admitted to the college and thereby received an invitation to live with her mother's cousin. This arrangement lasted through her first year of college, and suited Irena and Sophia well. She was making progress in her academics and the family was proud of her, as it bode well for a suitable marital prospect, such as Mae had procured.

It was during the second summer of her liberation from parental control that she met Efren's father; the dashing, dancing Osario, who was a salesman of sorts, on holiday at the resort. It was Osorio who beguiled her with his flashing smile and charming ways, and interrupted her carefully planned future. Her days off were spent with him, swimming and picnicking, along with much affectionate talk while lolling about on the cool green grass of a nearby meadow. Inevitably, after her work shift ended, there were many passionate nights of heated caresses which eventually resulted in amorous bouts of lusty love-making. It was during one of these bouts in the meadow under the spell of a brilliant full moon that the tiny speck that was to become Efren, was duly selected by the product of Osario's rapture to be fertilized and sent on its way to plant itself in Irena's young and fertile womb. Thus was Irena's and Osario's life changed forever and thus did Efren's begin. An inheritance of passionate appetites, weak resolve and obsessive self gratification living within him from the start, along with a good dose of arrogance regarding his future success with women and the tango.

The woman in his arms made a sudden move into him, as she was jostled on the dance floor. It startled him, and he looked down at her reassuringly and created a dance pattern that would take them into the flow of the other dancers. She responded to his maneuver, and he was satisfied that she noticed nothing of his mental departure. Annoyed a bit at the interruption, he allowed himself to return to his thoughts. What would his Mama's life have been like had she not sacrificed herself at the altar of her passions at such an inopportune time? What would his own life be like if he hadn't had to leave Argentina at such a tender age, and in such a hurry. It seems that life was full of "if-only this" and "if only that." But, Efren thought, the truth was if Sara had been more understanding and less demanding, and hadn't threatened his well-fortressed ego, things might have been completely different. Efren guarded that ego very carefully, as it took years to rebuild after his mother's constant barrages, using her ability to keep him off center with her illnesses. It became an endless chore for him to maintain his equilibrium and to keep other women at a safe distance emotionally because of his fear of rejection and abandonment. Yet, the warmth and passion of the woman he was dancing with enticed and excited him. He noticed himself tense at the thought, and inadvertently, he tightened his hold on her. He allowed himself to smile down at her inquisitive languid eyes, and it was at that moment he realized that this fragile, delicate, vulnerable woman reminded him of Sara.

As the realization hit him, he became aware that their tango had ended. The American woman murmured something and turned to go, but he reached for her arm and with the utmost charm, requested another dance. Though he risked leading her on because of her past obsession with him, he knew that he was on to something significant in the puzzle of his life, and that with the recollection of his conversation with his Aunt and what his mother had told him, the pieces were beginning to fit together in his mind. As usual, dancing the tango cleared a path upon which to set his thoughts. The American woman smiled up at him, accepting his invitation for yet another dance, probably gratefully, he thought. Well, he was grateful too. He took her hand, once again drawing her to himself, and as the music began the two disparate dancers became one in motion; once again dipping and weaving to the music, each visiting their own mental and emotional interiors while supporting one another's momentary needs.

The woman seemed pleased by his request, and Efren allowed his thoughts to return to the plight of his Mama. It didn't seem fair. How ironic it is that the imprudent decisions we make, even though borne of love, can come back to haunt us and destroy our dreams. How fragile our lives are when little twists of fate can derail us and put us into uncharted territory, lost and bereft, trying in vain to resuscitate our best-laid plans. Efren could imagine his Mama's panic when by the second month after their passionate summer, it became clear that she was carrying Osario's child. Her chances of completing her education and succeeding in her future plans were over. Osario was told, a wedding planned, and quickly. It would never do for her parents to suspect anything. Her wedding dreams that had once brought her shivers of anticipation were gone forever. No white silk gown covered with iridescent sequins, no veiled crown, no hundreds of guests bringing mountains of richly decorated presents. The arrangements were made hastily and in such a way as to assuage any suspicions regarding the sudden nuptials. A small family wedding in the village church, and off they went on the manufactured story of a business trip that Osario was bidden to take. In the end, they pulled it off, and nobody bothered to question the early arrival of Efren upon their return. Large babies ran in the family, it was said.

After Efren was born, life changed drastically for Irena and Osorio, as it does for most married couples. The time that Irena once had for Osario was now spent on the baby. Efren's father, feeling ignored and unimportant, retreated to the haven of his office earlier each day, and to the romance of the tango by night, dancing well into the morning, which left Irena feeling more and more neglected herself. But she had Efren, and with his hearty appetite and demanding cries monopolizing more and more of her time, she became less and less concerned about her husband's absences. However, not enough to replace the feeling of his arms around her and the longing she had to rekindle the tender closeness they once had together.

It must have been then, Efren surmised, that she discovered through her loneliness and creeping depression that if she took to her bed, she got immediate concern and attention from him and the others. Her mother always helped with the baby during these bouts, and even Osario became more attentive—he brought her flowers, and once, an impulsive gift of beautifully matched pearls. Mae came to the rescue with meals, and sisterly advice for recovery. It always lifted Irena's spirits to be catered to, and she used the ruse many times as Efren grew up. He soon learned the drill and responded to her illnesses as all the others did—with concern and trepidation.

In Efren's mind, the ill wind blowing away his mother's reason brought with it a gift of good. He and his father began to bond with their collaboration of sorts, which sought to keep some semblance of familial normalcy in the home. Fate smiled on him, and his father who had not related at all to baby Efren began a whole new relationship with the young adolescent Efren. This was, after all, his son—his only child and heir. Curiously, though Irena thought he could do no wrong, she began to resent the gradual decline of Osario's attention as his focus shifted from her needs to his son's. Their arguments escalated. The evenings began innocently enough— Osario came home, dinner was served, the day was discussed, etc. But after he was sent to bed, he could hear his mother and father talking, quietly at first, and then louder and louder. Then he would hear the heavy creaking of the stairs, echoing their footfalls as they stomped up angrily, followed by the sounds slamming doors. They no longer slept in the same room.

As he entered upper school, he finally realized that his mother's drinking was getting out of hand. The little glass of sherry he used to share with her after dinner became two glasses, and then three. She became petulant and accusing, her words slurring as she berated Osario about his peregrinations to the tango clubs around town . . . each night a different club . . . each morning returning as dawn was breaking. Efren dreaded hearing the tirade that would follow his return, his mother well fortified by her new drink of choice, Ginebra. First it was orange juice laced with Ginebra, and then, straight Ginebra in a glass of ice. Clear, strong and potent, it soon held her in its sinister grip.

Upon reaching his senior year, his studies were pre-empted more and more often by calls to the bedside of his now deteriorating Mama, and he began to notice the gauntness of her frame and the glassiness of her eyes as her mind became vapid with the slow agony of alcoholic dementia. Her copious consumption of alcohol, along with actual and imagined bouts of illness and withdrawal added years to her face. Her once luxurious hair was wispy and lifeless, clinging to her head like the hair on one of the shrunken heads he had read about at school. It both frightened and disgusted him, and as Efren paced the floor by her bedside that day, he came to two conclusions: first, the day would come when his mother would not survive her addiction, and secondly, he could survive in a man's world as his father did, without losing himself to anyone.

Surprisingly, his mama survived that particular bout of malaise, but he had not. Emotionally, the scenario was wearing thin. To add to his problems, his father was tense, distracted, and not around very much so his mama depended more and more on her son. One night, she had so much to drink that he was afraid she couldn't make it up the stairs, and so he had to put her to bed. He winced as he remembered the embarrassment of that night. He had returned very early in the morning from one of his favorite tango clubs. It was a warm summer dawn, just before he went away to the University. He hadn't met Sara yet, and he had many girls on the string who were happy to spend an hour or so in his company dancing the tango and later, spending another hour or so in his little roadster, parked at the top of the hill talking and making love while they watched the dawn come up over the city. When he finally came home, tiptoeing up the porch steps much like his father, he encountered Irena who was waiting up for him, drunk as usual, bitter and accusing. He didn't even think she knew whether she it was him or his father. He tried to calm her, taking her arm. "I'm sorry I upset you, Mamacita", he said, "Please now, let's get you to bed." As he proceeded to guide her up the stairs, she railed at him with each step, her words slurring, arms flailing. As they reached the last step, her legs gave way and she crumpled into his arms. He managed to get her into her bedroom, and as he sat her on the edge of the bed and swung her legs up, she fell back suddenly—her legs slipped out of his grasp, and her skirt went flying and landed like a heap of rags atop her wrinkled belly. He was mortified at having to witness this indignity, and quickly set her skirts in order, pulled off her shoes one by one, and pulled the covers up. She was already snoring as he slipped quietly out of the room, fighting back the tears. From that night forward, the wall went up, carefully constructed to keep him safe forevermore from female intrusion. His mother had been enough of a drain on him and now that she was deteriorating so rapidly, he began subconsciously to buttress himself against his imminent loss with numerous and meaningless sexual escapades. He disdained the use of alcohol; he was too smart for that. However, he began to be seen with his father at the clubs, and he decided to immerse himself in the tango. He would watch the men at those clubs—how they would get a woman to dance with them with just a small nod of the head, and later he would see them leaving with one of the women, and sometimes two.

And so, life went on for those three: his father in his own world of business by day and tango clubs by night, Efren studying earnestly for his exams and developing his machismo with the tango and tango women, and Mama Irena in an alcoholic stupor, getting more anemic and sickly each day, always complaining and raging on about the state of her life and the man she chose to live it with. The day came when Efren received his letter of acceptance from the University, and they all celebrated. He and his father were hopeful as Irena regained her health and remained sober for a time. That is until he began seeing Sara, and the events that occurred on the evening of "the Sara incident." After his return from Miami, the same old demons inhabited his mama with only a brief respite when he got his first job as an apprentice draftsman at one of the large civil engineering firms in downtown Buenos Aires. Sara was, by then, on tour with a new tango show, receiving rave notices for her prodigious talent and elegant style with the dance. He was so proud of her, and though he missed her, life was simpler at home now that she was gone. In fact, his life was relatively manageable, though not very exciting. And then, his mama slipped and fell after another drinking bout, and once again, her health deteriorated even more seriously. He remembered clearly the day that he was called from work, and he had the feeling he would be going to his mama's bedside for the last time.

As he entered her room and his father came to embrace him, he knew by the expression on his father's face that this was the end of the line for his wife. He didn't want to look at his mama, afraid of what he would see. He took a deep breath and turned to face the bed. Her stillness took his breath away. There was no form under the covers—they were as flat as if there was nothing but air under them. There on the pillow was a small, old face; its weary mouth set in a thin lipped grimace. She seemed suspended in time, barely breathing, and only vaguely aware of the people staring at her shrunken form. She drifted in and out of consciousness, but during one brief lucid moment, she was able to lock her eyes on her son, whom she could still subjugate to her will. He would never forget her penetrating gaze as she held his hand and drew him near for the last time. Her hand was cold in his, and he shuddered as it suddenly grew limp and her life slipped away, leaving them all standing there with their tears and regrets. Yet he felt a strange sense of detachment as he carefully placed his mama's hand by her side and reached up gently to close her eyes, still fixed on his. As he shut them, he shut it all out, and felt liberated for the first time in his life. He knelt by the bed for a time, and then he left, not knowing what he was feeling, as though in a dream. He would get through the burial in the tiny cemetery by the church, and with each passing day, more and more clarity came about his relationship with mama. He faced the fact that though he saw through her manipulation of him, he knew she loved him. The conversation with Aunt Mae verified that. He also knew that she was a weak and fragile person, and he owned up to the fact that he allowed the bondage he experienced because he loved the captor. She was the one woman whom he knew he could always make happy . . . always. But, what about other women? He had no idea. He only knew that now his mama was gone, and he was going to rebuild his life. He had a good job, and enjoyed his routine. It was typical of the Argentine lifestyle: get up in the morning, go to work, work, get off work, go home, take a nap, clean up, go out for dinner around ten p.m., and then on to a tango club. Each night, a different club was "the place to be seen", and the dancers all showed up at midnight and danced for hours. It was a banquet of sorts, offering food for the soul in the form of tango love and intrigue wrapped up in an exotic package which he unwrapped each night with relish.

Sara came back into his life one night at one of the clubs—probably a Tuesday at La Estrella. She was by now the best and most beautiful tango dancer in all of Buenos Aires. They soon became each other's steady partner, and he recalled with pride the ease with which he beat out the other tangueros. The lessons he had taken paid off in spades for him, and Sara knew as he did that they were meant to be together forever. However, forever didn't last very long—only until Sara's next tour. It was one of the last balmy nights of summer when he entered the outdoor dance floor of the club that Sunday. The floor was surrounded by little lights twinkling in the breeze. He remembered the smell of jasmine in the air, and as he waited for his Ginebra at the bar, he turned at the sound of laughter, and saw a group of people sitting at a table with a buxom, brassy dark haired girl who was the center of attention. He observed her style—sassy and sexy—and as she saw him watching her, she flirted with him openly. He smiled and nodded for her to dance with him, and one thing led to another. They became quite a pair—sometimes having fun and entertaining each other and sometimes at each other's throats, thereby provoking much talk and entertainment for their friends. After a time, he moved out of his father's home and into Lupita's apartment across town—a move he would soon regret.

As he and the American woman danced on, Efren began to tire of his mental journey. He once again turned his attention to the tango. How he loved it! He had become so good that the numerous women who longed to dance with him would try to position themselves around the edge of the dance floor, trying to get him to notice them. Glancing around the room, he could see several of his admirers waiting for the music to end so that they could at last have a chance to partner him. But, the American woman was good too, and he had enjoyed his time with her. He liked the way she followed him and how compliant she was in his arms. As they danced, he could sense her pleasure in the figures he chose to lead, and how he executed them so that their bodies synchronized perfectly with the music. And now, he could tell that the music was ending. What to do? He knew he was getting to the edge with this woman. As a matter of tango protocol, a man never asked for a third dance with the same woman unless there was more to his intentions than to dance with her. At home in Argentina, some clubs played sets of five dances, and if the woman excused herself after the third or fourth dance, the man was insulted. But in America, and at most of the workshops such as this one, dance sets weren't used, and two dances was the limit. Knowing this woman's penchant for romanticizing any undue attention he gave her, yet not ready to let her go, he took a chance by casually chatting with her about the weather during the transition between songs, and then as the music began he said "Listen . . . it's the new Pugliesi tango . . . one of my favorites!", and before she could protest (as if she would) he took her to him once more, avoiding her inquisitive glance.

As the music hit a crescendo, his thoughts once again invaded his mind, and up came "the scene", the one that rankled his memory and caused the hairs on the back of his neck to bristle. He and Lupita had just returned from a rather pleasant Sunday at the lake. They were back at the apartment, and she was in the kitchen cleaning up the breakfast dishes, as they had slept late and left everything on the table in their haste to leave early in order to catch as much of the warm sunshine as possible. Lupita hated to do that, and now she was in a surly mood. The plan was to come home and rest a bit, shower and dress for dinner out and an evening of tango dancing. But the phone had rung. Efren answered it and heard the voice at the other end telling him there had been a horrible accident. Sara was seriously injured—near death. "Oh God! Where? How? I'll be right there. Tell her." As he jotted down the location of the hospital, his heart beat rapidly. He felt hot and sick, and the lines on his forehead deepened. The folds around his mouth drooped and he turned ashen as he hung up the receiver and said to Lupita; "It's Sara. There's been an accident. I'm going to her."

Efren know that Lupita was jealous of Sara. Though he knew she was aware of their past relationship, he managed to assuage Lupita's suspicions by his flattery and charm, swearing that it was over between them. Everyone knew that Lupita had a hot temper, and he took care to keep things as above board and smooth as possible in order to avoid being the object of one of her famous tirades. He did his best to hide his anxiety as he explained his distress at the ominous news, and took his jacket to leave, saying he would return as soon as he could. He could still picture Lupita as he left, standing there with her hands on her hips, eyes narrowed accusingly, and before she could object he hastily turned and ran down the stairs. Efren knew he would pay for this later, but for now, all he could think of was Sara.

As he drove to the hospital, he suddenly grew weary. How much more could he be expected to take? All the women in his life wanted something from him. His mother, Lupita, Sara, even the lovers he paid for—they all wanted a piece of him, and he had none left to give them. Of course, Sara really needed him now, and he knew that. She, above all was not a game-player. As it turned out, the accident had been a serious one. She had been pinned under the vehicle in which she was riding with some of the other members of the tango troupe. Her partner had been in no condition to drive as they left a cast party after the performance that night, but her offer to drive had been refused. When the car rolled over three times after Andre failed to negotiate a sudden curve, Sara ended up crushed under the front end of the car. Andre managed to escape with some badly banged up bones and minor injuries, probably due to his relaxed condition. He was able to crawl out of the window and summon a passing motorist, and he knew enough to call Efren.

The memory of the gripping fear he felt when he arrived at the hospital returned . . . the fear that Sara was dead. He paced in the waiting room for several hours, and when the doctor came he was relieved to hear that she was at least alive! Alive but maimed . . . a broken back and ribs. It had been necessary to put a rod in her back, but luckily no nerves or vertebrae were damaged, though it would be at least a year before it could be determined whether or not she would ever dance the tango again. Efren sat heavily into the chair and put his head in his hands.

When Efren returned to Lupita's apartment several days later, she received the news with outward concern, camouflaging her hidden joy. He could see through her ruse, and knew that she would be gloating, thinking that she would have him all to herself—dancing the tango and making love, while his Sara would be laying in bed immobile for an indefinite length of time. He began to turn the tables on Lupita; to spend less and less time with her, and took every chance he could to be at Sara's side. He loved going to her, and being there for her . . . being the one she looked forward to seeing every day. They talked and talked, and grew closer than ever before, and Efren loved re-living the moment a year after the surgery when Sara surprised him, coming to him unsteadily as he opened the door to her room and falling into his arms. Before long, through sheer will and determination, she was even able to dance a little with him, and he began sharing more and more of his time and life with her once again. It enthralled him to know that Sara had been reborn under his guidance and attentions—a new creation—and that she had come to depend on him for her physical and emotional sustenance. He had worked with her diligently, and it was under his urgings that she learned to walk, and then at last to dance! It was a long process, taking the better part of a year, but his patience paid off—in the smiles of gratitude she gave him, as well as in the bedroom.

However, as his happiness with Sara increased, Lupita was becoming a real problem. He felt guilt all right, and he didn't blame her for her daily tirades about his absences and worse, his lack of desire for intimacy. Just like his mama, she had trapped him. But this time, there were no family ties to bind him. He wanted a way out, and he wanted it fast. It came to him from Lupita herself one night when her rage against him welled up inside her and she turned on him with a fury. She grabbed the first thing she could and hurled the heavy leaded glass ashtray at him like a missile. Fortunately, her aim was bad and though it flew dangerously close to his head, it merely grazed his temple and shattered a cherished lamp on the table behind him. It was the final scene between them—the one which convinced him that it was time to leave Argentina, at least for a while, and to seek a new life away from the complications of his mishandled affairs.

Like an answer to prayer, he received a letter from the Los Angeles Tango Association announcing their plans for a "Fabulous three days of Tango classes and dancing in Isla Linda, a beautiful resort on a lush peninsula in the Western Caribbean. Would he consider attending and writing a poem for the invitation?" What timing! What good fortune! An opportunity to escape and to explore new territory with the added benefit of improving his Tango technique. A way to leave the cold Argentine winter for the sunny climes of the Gulf of Mexico. He might even extend his trip for a week or so. Chances are Lupita would have no qualms in bidding him good riddance, given her present state of mind, and Sara . . . well, at least Sara was dancing again. He felt exonerated having given her so much of himself in expediting her recovery. He was certain he loved her, up to a point, and he would assure her that he would take up their life together after the conference. She would not have to know whether he had other plans or not. He was certain she didn't really know how deep his involvement was with Lupita. In fact, she had convinced herself that the affair was just dalliance for him, and she told him that Lupita's hot temper and tumultuous nature would eventually drive him away. She had been proven right, of course, but now she expected him to give her all of his time. He was finally able to leave by saying that he needed to learn the newest tango techniques, and he promised to teach her all the dance figures he would learn and all the gossip he would hear at the workshop upon his return. Sara knew a lot of members of the teaching staff, and in fact had danced with many of them in shows. Efren would have to be careful about his extra-curricular activities, as reports might come back to her. Was there no end to his troubles?

But, the ruse had worked. He recalled the tremendous sense of freedom he felt as he boarded the plane, waving through the tiny window at Sara as her figure began to diminish with the rising of the plane. He relished the exhilaration he felt at the prospect of a new experience, and he no longer felt trapped. He hadn't felt so much freedom since long before he could remember, and the workshop did not disappoint him, so far, that is.

Efren sensed the end of the haunting melody he had been dancing to was imminent. He allowed himself one last realization before letting go of this partner. He had learned three important things from his mental visit to the past: First, things appear different when seen from a distance than they do up close: second, his feelings for Sara went deeper than he thought, but it was difficult for him to maintain a relationship with only one woman, and third, it's not possible for people to escape from their choices in life, because if any resulting situations go unresolved, they just follow one to the next locale, where they resurface in other situations. This woman he was dancing with . . . would she demand a piece of him too? The music ended, and as if reading his thoughts, she looked up at him winsomely, smiled, and thanked him for the dances. Mi Dios, he thought, here it comes. But then, he was thrown off guard. A remarkable change took place in their relationship as she drew away from him. It occurred to him that while he was reminiscing and sorting out his difficulties during their dances, this woman, whom he had dominated throughout their acquaintance had suddenly become confident—immune to his considerable charm. Yes, she was standing up to him now, and suddenly she seemed amazingly attractive to him. She was almost regal—cool and graceful. And he had not noticed before what a lovely color her eyes were—an unusual deep, dark blue.

As he was about to speak, she quickly said goodnight; and as she turned to leave through the swinging doors, he noticed her swaying hips, and as her scent caught his nostrils, they flared almost imperceptibly as he fought the urge to follow her out.

*　　*　　*

Figure Three

LA CRUZADA
(The Cross)

In this provocative tango move, when a man executes La Cruzada, he leads the woman backwards for two steps, and on the third, he moves toward her and turns her in such a manner that her feet must cross. This causes a break in the rhythm and momentum of their dance, at which time, the man can contemplate and create his next move. Similarly, the crosses that inevitably enter our lives, will break our rhythm and momentum, and cause us to have to make critical decisions. To further compound our difficulties, it's a fact that these crosses never occur at an appropriate time. However if we trust the process, we will use the interruptions they create to develop a strategy for our next moves. In life as in the tango, those moves can stall us indefinitely, or allow us to uncross our feet and move on.

The little girl giggled and squealed as her grandpapa spun her around on the gritty linoleum dance floor. A sprightly tango was playing on the old Victrola, cracking and hissing with every revolution, the needle dulling itself in the well-worn grooves. They twirled and swirled, the old tanguero and his protégé, as he led her through the figures of a popular Milonga. His hands held both of hers, her feet on top of his, and then as she tried in vain to match his stride, her feet left his and she became airborne for a moment, laughing as she landed, begging for more.

The room in which they danced was long and narrow. There was a small stage at the far end for a guitarist and the impassioned tango singers who came on Saturday nights to sing for drinks. Square tables topped with checkered tablecloths held vases of plastic poppies and salt and pepper shakers with rusted tops. In the open windows sat pots of live geraniums, sunning themselves in the lingering light of a beautiful summer afternoon. The walls were lined with so many pictures that the yellowed wallpaper barely peeked out between them. The variously colored miss-matched frames hung in uneven rows, displaying stained newspaper clippings touting the past glories of the little tango bar, along with autographed pictures of various tango dancers and singers who had performed there before success and notoriety overcame them. These celebrities shared the walls with several photos of Eva Peron, as well as the most famous and beloved tango singer in all of Argentina: Carlos Gardel.

It was Sunday again, and little Sara loved Sundays. Her grandparents owned the tango bar in the town of La Boca; a tourist magnet for its quaint and colorful storefronts and colony of artists and dancers. For as long as Sara could remember, every Sunday after church, her Mama, Papa and two younger brothers would climb into the old Chevy truck for the drive to La Boca where her grandparents lived. The boys rode in the back of the truck, and Sara sat up front on her Mama's lap. It was a long, bumpy ride across town from the church, but once they arrived—even before they turned into the side yard and parked—the smell of home-made empenadas and barbecued chicken wafted out through the screen of the creaky screen door, beckoning them into the dark interior. Oh, the wonderful smells! The food, Grandmama's perfume, Grandpapa's cigars, and the scent of old wood and whiskey blended themselves together with the familiar sounds of the perennial tangos, and tattooed themselves indelibly on Sara's heart, soul and mind.

When Sara was just three years old, she would sit on her Grandpapa's lap after a sumptuous Sunday dinner, and they would listen together to the old Victrola. They played the old Tango songs, and as Gardel sang soulfully of love and anguish, her Grandpapa would sing with him, and then tell her of the stories in the songs. Yes, all the songs of love . . . the tender love of a man for a woman, a woman for a man, and of humanity's endless and seemingly fruitless search for true love and the meaning of life. Love in bloom, love gone wrong, love for a lifetime, love for the moment, love out of control, and love for sale. The words expressed much about the matter of love and its suffering and joy, and as Sara grew older, it gave her a perspective that most of the young girls her age did not have. That may have accounted for the fact that she became more or less isolated from her peers. That, and the fact that young ladies of "good breeding" were not allowed to dance the tango in Argentina, for it was considered controversial—too sensual and worldly. While Sara was developing her intimacy with the tango, her contemporaries spent their lives in an insular world: going to private schools and attending teas and other well-chaperoned social functions with their mamas, aunts, cousins and godmothers. Sara enjoyed setting herself apart from the giggly, awkward girls that inhabited her world, as she knew she was special and different, and could feel her own beauty and grace. She possessed a self-confidence in the power she had over her body as she executed the intricate tango patterns with her grandfather. He shared her love of the tango, and brought her innocently into it. She was the only girl, born smack in the middle of four boys, and from the beginning, stayed away from their boisterous activities. From an early age, she preferred playing quietly with her dolls, listening to classical music on the little record player in her grandmama's room. She loved Lecuona, whose fiery, poetic tangos moved her spirit from the start. Her grandfather stood in the doorway and watched as she would dance her dollies around the room, giving them the lessons he had taught her, applauding wildly at each move. She never tired of the charade, and then she would put another tango on the player and dance in front of the big mahogany framed mirror on its own special stand. She collected tango postcards of exotic dancing women and their tangueros, and as she watched her image in the mirror, she would strike the dramatic poses from the figures on the cards, practicing the attitudes and facial expressions as well, until she was ready to take on another lesson. Her grandpapa would hold out his arm for her to take, and the two of them would go grandly down the stairs into the little Tango bar; the old man and his willing pupil.

When Sara was very little, she began learning the tango by dancing on the tops of Grandpapa's shoes: forward, side, back, and back together. Soon she learned the steps and could do them herself, dancing in front of him, as she learned to feel the music and follow his lead, all the while holding her arms up, looking at him adoringly. Forward, side, back, then step back and cross. Ah, "La Cruzada". The cross. And her little feet crossed so prettily. She would place them just so, her blue eyes waiting for his praise.

Then, just before her fifteenth birthday, the image in the mahogany-framed mirror began to change. Her recalcitrant puberty finally caught up with her, and curves replaced the straight lines of her body. Suddenly, different emotions surfaced and she became a stranger to herself, giving her yearnings she couldn't explain. While her girlfriends turned to flirting with boys, Sara suppressed her emerging romantic thoughts. Embarrassed and confused, she poured out all those energies and the deepest feelings of her heart into her dancing. She took lessons from a tango maestro who was amazed at her abilities, and this fulfilled her for a time. Rather than run with the crown of her peers, she preferred to spend her time with adults, joining in their conversations about the weather, soccer games, and even politics. Thus she gained the name "Ice Queen" from her contemporaries, and was thought to be aloof, and to consider herself above them. Which she was, of course.

Her brothers were of no help at all. They teased her constantly and nicknamed her "heartbreaker from hell", as she successfully quashed the amorous efforts of her would-be suitors. They longed for her attentions, and she bewitched them. Willowy and slim, elegant and lithe, she had a long, graceful neck that supported a lovely face with full lips and amazingly blue eyes. Her hair was the color of spun honey. She was long limbed and nimble-footed with a beautiful turn to her ankles as she walked. When she danced, her steps were sinewy, sensuous, stalking. She drew you into the dance in such a way that in watching, it seemed as though you were in her body—one with her movement—feeling her ecstasy. It created an intimacy with her that belied her emotional naiveté.

As time passed, her parents began to worry about her disinterest in normal teenage activities. Her stern father, in particular, voiced his disapproval and wished for her to engage in more academic pursuits. But all he had to do was watch her dance, and even he became mesmerized in the way that she executed her steps. It was indeed a beautiful sight to see. She would glide along the floor as though she danced on a sliver of air, which she had put in captivity under her feet. Her "figure eights" would roll out like mercury finding its own level, resting in just the right spot, gracing the grit of that old linoleum floor as if it were the finest imported marble.

Inevitably, one sunny afternoon at the little tango bar, a celebrated tango master, having heard of her legendary beauty and grace, came in to watch, and then asked to dance with her. Sara was always dancing with the regular patrons of the establishment, and as the stranger approached, he did so with such felicity and confidence that she trustingly acquiesced to dance with him. As she entered into the circle of his arms and submitted to his lead, she could tell then, that this was different. She knew immediately that this man was as much a part of the tango as she was, and that the tango compelled him as it did her. As they began to dance, he took her with him into the soul of the music, swirling through the molinetes and ochos that she had known since her childhood. He led her impeccably, so that she followed easily, adding her own flashes and flourishes of footwork with such spirit and elegance that it took his breath away. "Eso, eso," he said. "Yes, yes, Bravo!" It was a defining moment for both of them. One of those rare events that brings with it the realization that life from then on would be forever changed, and they both felt the magic of the inevitability of it all. Sara felt a shiver travel through her body and nodded in agreement as the stranger asked to speak with her parents. Her heart pounding, she watched as they led the maestro to a table along the wall, right under the picture of a smiling Eva Peron, smiling down on them like a patron saint.

They were speaking to each other in earnest tones, all the while punctuating their sentences with glances at Sara. This both caused her anxiety and aroused her curiosity deliciously. What could they be saying?

In all of her 12 years on earth, nothing this remarkable had ever happened to Sara. She was born in the late 1940's, her mama's third child. Her two older rough-and-tumble brothers welcomed their little fair-haired sister with the kewpie-doll lips and beautiful eyes. She had a sweetness about her and a sunny nature that sat on the surface of a troubled soul, for Sara had a yearning in her heart which none could satisfy. Not her mama nor her brothers, nor her father, who sternly admonished her moodiness. His Germanic roots invaded his better sense more often than not, and caused a rift between himself and his daughter. While he was kind at times, and always protective of Sara and her mother, he exercised an iron will over them when it came to life in general, and when he became annoyed or displeased, he became cold and overbearing, and there was no reasoning with him. The boys fared better, and were already developing an attitude of superiority over the females of the household. They all, however, favored Sara and looked after her with grave concern.

As to her relationship with her grandpapa, Sara's father was not entirely comfortable with their closeness. Especially when it came to the tango. Being non-artistic and a pragmatist at that, their passion for the dance escaped him entirely. He felt powerless and completely left out of, and completely left out of their little world, and he was not used to that. As Sara grew, their increasing enthusiasm for each other's company became even more unacceptable, as he felt his power completely waning in his influence over her. Naturally, this gave Sara a wonderful excuse to escape from his control of her. She loved the tango even more for that escape, and though he attempted more than once to reason with her about a pursuit of academics and intellectual growth, she managed to elude the discussion. He desperately wanted her to attend the University, but she was able to skirt the issue skillfully, and took secret notice of the gleam in his eyes on the rare occasion when she saw him watching her dance. She knew she was good, and knew that he knew she was good, and this dichotomy became a bone of contention between them. The maestro in the tango bar was just another competitor to her father's plan for her, as well as for the attentions of his Sara, truth be told. But now, Sara would have none of his notion of a mundane existence in the world of books and boring exams. She strained to listen to the new man in her life the man whose hands held the world she desired.

But, just now her father was gesturing angrily at her mother, her grandfather and the stranger. Her stomach took a turn, as she saw her dreams drifting out of her reach, blown away by the hissing words of her father. She began to pray for her deliverance to Saint Teresa, the little flower who brought her through all the frights and frictions of her life thus far. As her tears began welling up, the miracle took place. Abruptly, her father turned silent and Sara was called over to her family and the stranger. In her desperation and relief, she failed to notice that her miracle had transferred her tears to her father's anguished eyes. She would remember this day as the turning point in her life. The point at which her life would change forever. Out of the cocoon of her childhood she would emerge, opening her wings of escape. Those wings which would take her on a journey that would overwhelm her at times and haunt her days and nights with unsettling but exquisite demands on her emotions and abilities. But for now, she was just a little girl with a big dream and a miraculous turn of events.

Wide-eyed and wondrous, Sara strained to hear her fate as the two men talked and caught snatches of sentences and words being bantered across the room between the maestro, (whom she discovered was named Senor Alejandro Bautista) and her father. From Senor ". . . personally train her" Her father: . . . "her studies at school must be continued." Answer: "yes, yes, of course." And then . . . "trust fund for college." Senor Bautista: . . . "as if she were my own daughter, and I promise you will have her home for the summer." Her father pressed the advantage; "I will only sign these papers if they state that my daughter will be chaperoned at all times by a woman of whom I approve." Senor Bautista nodded; "Yes, yes, I will see to it personally." "One more thing: I don't want her touring until she has finished her secondary education." Sara caught that, all right. Touring? Away from Buenos Aires? She thought she heard the Senor mention London, and Paris. Could this really be happening? She remembered reading about such countries in a book at school. Then, she heard Senor Bautista speak very softly and convincingly, and her hopes soared as she sensed her father's gradual change of heart. "I can assure you I want nothing to happen to your daughter. She will be trained by the best, and God be willing, one day your child will be a true star of the tango stage. Think what that will do for her future, and what it will provide for her education" This, he knew would seal the bargain, and he was right. Then as her father was signing the papers proffered by the maestro, her mother fluttered in with a plate of warm pastries and hot coffee. She stood by Sara and took her hand, giving it a conspiratory squeeze. Thus the impossible became possible, and the little girl was on the brink of living her big dream. As the dream became reality however, as dreams eventually do, she would find it was a big leap from the gritty little linoleum floor to the bright lights of the tango stage.

Sara gained recognition during those years for her skillful dancing as well as her beauty and charm. She could be moody, though, and the cast of the show learned to give her a wide berth when she thought her own performance was not up to the standards she set for herself. Her audiences loved her, but even that failed to convince her of her worth. A perfectionist, she would drive herself to the point of exasperation, and berate herself for not having the stamina to work that extra hour for mastering a figure or executing a difficult lift. She soon got the reputation for being difficult and moody, and her dance partners felt helpless at times to lift her or her mood. Still, she managed to charm them the next day, or at the next performance, and all was forgiven. Fortunately, she learned to survive her own opinion of herself, as she would need that quality for what lay ahead.

She arrived home after a successful tour in Paris on the eve of her eighteenth birthday. Senor Bautista, an honorable man, dismissed her from the troupe as agreed, and she was to enroll in the University the following week. Sara was greatly missed by her family, and they welcomed her with happy hearts. She felt warm and safe, and spent the evening talking around the table after one of her mama's sumptuous meals.

The next day, she awoke to her brother's rendition of her birthday song . . . loud and raucous as usual. It was good to be home, and that night, they feted her with a party in the little tango bar, inviting her many friends as well as some of theirs. The old Victrola played plaintive tango music and once again, tango feet shuffled across the linoleum floor, and Sara felt happy and light-hearted as she danced one, two, three, four tangos in a row with a line of ardent admirers, who had patiently waited their turn with her. She finally begged off, and went to sit on the patio, when one of her brothers introduced her to a friend from high school.

There was something in him that attracted her, though she wasn't sure what. He was very gallant, and just short of handsome. He had an air of intelligence and confidence, and as he took her hand and asked her to join him for a tango, her heart beat wildly. Of all the men she had dallied with during her time with the company, none had affected or interested her so deeply. Yet, they only had one dance, and soon the young man left the party without even saying goodbye to her. After a fitful night, she awoke to the delicious smell of breakfast cooking, and hastily put herself together to join the others at the kitchen table. "Alonso", she asked her brother, "who was that friend of yours I danced with at the party?" "Which one?", he asked. "Every time I saw you, you were dancing with someone!". "Oh, you know the one. You brought him to the patio. He was tall and dark; the strong, silent, brooding type." "Ah, Sara . . . that was Efren. But he has a girlfriend!"

The week passed quickly, and she was off to the University, having been accepted with some influence placed upon the president by his old friend, her father. He drove her there with great enthusiasm and satisfaction. He secretly believed that once she began her studies and met new, intellectually stimulating friends, she would forget all this nonsense with the tango. He convinced her that she should study Liberal Arts, and maybe turn her love for dance into becoming a teacher of small children, or so he hoped. As for Sara, it was difficult for her to say goodbye to Senor Bautista and the members of the troupe, but she knew she would be dancing with them again during the summers. She also had heard a rumor that Efren was also enrolling at the college, and oh, how she wanted to see him again. However, she knew better than to mention anything about Efren to her father.

On her third day at school, during a wait in line to change a class, a flush swept through her as she spotted Efren walking by. She waved a greeting to him, but he kept walking. "He didn't even remember me" she told herself. Then and there, she determined to find him and change that, and she did. It took her a month and much conniving, but she managed to check his schedule of classes and "run into him" during a blistery day of an early winter storm.

She seduced him easily, and eventually told him of that first meeting and dance in the tango bar, but as she suspected, he barely recalled the incident. Wisely, Sara made no issue of it, and mutually smitten, they began seeing each other often during that semester, and the following semester, spending hours together talking and laughing, pouring over their books and studying for exams. Their lovemaking was intense; deep and powerful yet leaving her feeling aimless and empty, for Efren could not commit, and though she tried, nothing Sara could do sexually or emotionally could break through his barriers. Yet, they were inseparable and spent much of their vacation time at home together, which concerned Sara's father a great deal.

He needn't have bothered, as it turned out, for at the end of Sara's freshman year she was dealt another devastating blow; one which would grieve her for many years. The word came that her beloved grandfather had passed, and she left for home immediately without being able to say goodbye to Efren, or to take her final exams.

When a close member of the family dies, everything changes. As Sara gazed through her tears at the lifeless face of her beloved grandfather, she had no idea of the series of events that were ahead for her, or how they would affect her for the rest of her life. For the surviving spouse, children and grandchildren will play an increasingly significant part of life. In her grandmother's case, the mourning and grief were diminished by the dire financial implications of the patriarch's passing. The tango bar could not continue as before, as he was the essence of its popularity. This meant that the profits it generated would no longer be there to take up the slack in the lives of the family. Though Sara's brothers were grown and working in the city, money was scarce, and their wives and children were often given needed help from the family business.

Many hours were spent talking around the kitchen table in the days following the simple funeral. Tango dancers from all the surrounding towns, who had spent many happy nights in the tango bar, revered its proprietor and came to pay him homage. They despaired the prospect of an era having ended, and their tango opportunities diminished. After many nights of family conversations, a consensus was reached. Something would have to be done immediately to prevent Sara's grandmother from having to leave her home, where she worked and cooked, cared for the grandchildren and felt useful and needed. It was Sara who decided that she would have to leave her studies and return to the performances which would bring in ample revenue to save the tango bar which her grandfather had so well established. The family gratefully accepted.

As crosses valiantly borne can also bring redemption, Sara's anguish at leaving Efren to his studies took a turn as her heart sang at the prospect of dancing again. Even during their last act of lovemaking the night before her departure, her thoughts kept her from complete surrender to the thrust of his ardor, and their parting was bittersweet and unsettling. She knew she might lose him, but she vowed she would never again lose her intimate involvement with the tango. Never!

And so, the years passed sweetly for Sara. The beauty of her dancing was only surpassed by her beauty of form and face. As her career ascended, she was in demand all over the world, and touring with the show resulted in more travels. She was acclaimed in Italy, Paris, Germany, and even did a royal performance for the Queen in England. Her finances grew with her popularity, and she was able to hire help to run the tango bar during her absences. And when she returned home between tours, there was always a big celebration and milonga to which tangueros and well-wishers came from as far away as Buenos Aires. Everyone wanted to see her dance, and to dance with her. Of course she was happy to see Efren as well, and they would dance like old times on the floor which was no longer gritty linoleum, but burnished wood with warm golden tones. As far as their relationship was concerned, Sara could tell that it had changed to friendship. She had also heard a rumor that he had a lover for the past few months, and there was talk of marriage. But though his coldness chilled her heart she avoided any thought of regret, and looked forward to getting back to her career.

The years passed like quicksilver. Efren graduated from the University, and was hired by an Engineering firm in Buenos Aires. Sara's career was at a peak, and her life was under control when fate once again stepped in and changed it all.

The evening started out on a good note. The final performance of "Tango Fantasia" had brought the audience to their feet with shouts of "Bravo!" Chants of *"Uno mas, uno mas!"* came tumbling up to the stage in waves, filling the ears of the bowing performers who happily danced one more encore for their adoring fans. As the final curtain descended, Sara decided to join the cast in a final night celebration at a favorite hangout, "El Tigre". She and some of the others piled into one of the cars and headed for the outskirts of town where the legendary tango singer and his wife had converted their humble home into a family restaurant where they barbecued delicious beef which filled the place with marvelous smells and magnificent music. It reminded her of the little tango bar back home and her grandpapa, and how his love and encouragement had brought her this far. It was a perfect place for a celebration, and as the cast entered the crowded room, shouts of welcome and applause greeted them.

Maybe it was the sadness of her reverie about her grandfather, or the letdown of the final performance, but Sara felt strangely out of sorts and not in the mood for the Ginebra or beer that was being poured. As the old tango singer and his wife would sing a familiar song, everyone would join in, amid numerous toasts. Sara began to notice that her partner and the driver of the car, Reynaldo was on, at her count, his fourth Ginevre, and called to him over the din: "It's getting late, Reynaldo . . . let's go." "Silencio, Sara. I'm not about to leave a party in the middle of such fun. It's just getting started!" "I have a headache, amor. It's the smoke, and the noise. Please, take me back to the hotel, or I'll go with someone else. Besides, you've had enough gin for three people. Come on!" "OK, all right." He gulped the last of the fast acting liquor, and they rounded up the others and left the bar, still singing and laughing, except for Sara, though she did her best to join in. It was not until all of them were in the car and the driver turned to speak to her that she realized his words were slurred.

Sometimes, when the unthinkable is taking place, many thoughts flash through your head. "Why did I let this happen to me?"

"Why didn't I stop him?" "I knew I should have left earlier." "Why didn't I listen to myself?" On and on you think and ask these questions, but no answers come and it doesn't matter anyway. No amount of reasoning and questioning can change what happened.

Perhaps ten minutes after their departure, on a curve covered by loose gravel, the car spun wildly out of control, rolled several times, and Sara's next memory was of ascending towards a brilliant light amid a feeling of total peace. Then, without warning, there was total blackness and a soundless void whereupon she lost all sense of being. Her next memory was a feeling of relentless pain as she awoke in a hospital bed a week later.

Slowly, the agony of discovery began regarding the seriousness of her condition and the tragedy of the accident. Only she and Reynaldo survived, burdened with the guilt of surviving while the others died. What would life expect of them—of her—in repayment? Too much—it was just too much for her to think about. And then, though she fought it, she would sink back into the velvety blackness of nothingness where the pain of remembering held no sway.

It would be two more days before Sara allowed herself to awaken, still in pain and sorrow, but with a renewed determination to survive. As she struggled out of the misty depths of unconsciousness, the gray blue of a vaguely familiar face came into focus. It was Efren! Efren her friend and lover who had once adored her and made her life so worth living. Yes, the same Efren who dallied with countless courtesans and broke her heart more than once. Yet, there he was, smiling and warm with his touch on her cheek. "Oh, Efren, look at me! Why have you come now? I've wanted you so much, and when I could give you all that I was, you were gone. And now that I'm broken and helpless, you're here. Just go!" And through her tears, a final cry: "Go away!" But Efren just smiled and said with tenderness; "I'm not going. Sara, you have no idea what it will take to recover from your injuries. It's my chance to offer myself to you. I know I can never be the man that I should, or what you deserve, but you must accept me for what I can be." As she stared at the ceiling, she said "I understand, Efren. You're no worse than I am. We're not good for each other. Please give me peace and go!" But he would not leave. "Sorry, but I won't leave, Sara. You can cry all you want, but I won't leave. In time, you'll see the wisdom of it, and we'll both be the better for it. Now, get some sleep."

Indeed, Sara was the better for it and because of his care and her determination, her bones began to knit, and the muscles gradually gained back some of their strength. The doctor told her that as the car rolled, she was pushed into the dash from behind. The pressure was enough to jam her knee and thigh toward her back, dislocating her hip and shattering her femur. Following extensive surgery, after learning that the relocated hip was secured by a plate and screws, Sara went into fits of panic, followed by severe depression. She knew that even though she may be able to walk again, dancing might be out of the question. Out of the question? It was her life! She thought again of her grandfather—how they danced together—and she remembered his words; "You must always keep dancing, Sara. The tango fills the heart and enriches the soul. To be without the tango is to live with an empty heart." She would dance again.

Efren kept his promise, and stayed by her side, and after months of therapy, the day came when she was dismissed from the hospital. Wheeled out in her new chair, procured and decorated by Efren, she she was lifted gently into his waiting car. How bright the sun seemed, and it was good to feel the sweetness of the spring in the air. Her crutches were placed in the back seat and off they went; the bruised and battered little flower and her ubiquitous escort to the waiting warmth of the little tango bar and her family. How good it was to be home. How happy to see her family in these familiar surroundings after months of seeing them in that suffocating hospital room. Had she known that it would be two long years before she would dance again, she may not have had the strength to endure. During the first several months of her recovery, Efren couldn't do enough for her. He was caring, loving, protective and solicitous. He read to her, brought her food, and surprised her one day by bringing the old Victrola to her room so she could listen to tango music. Spoiled by her mother, her grandmother and even her father and brothers, she felt loved and doted on and encouraged, but nothing could replace that spot in her heart left empty and void of dancing. It drove her to work doggedly with her therapist, moving past the pain to make her joints and muscles once more do her bidding.

In time, as she grew stronger and more independent, Efren's interest and attention waned, as Sara knew it would. He began to depend more and more upon her grandmother to fill in for him until the day that blessed lady died. After a respectable period of time consoling Sara in her grief, he left her in the care of her now aging parents, and his visits grew even more seldom. Of course, he had a job, and she was very grateful and looked at him lovingly when he did visit. She suspected he had another new conquest, but she could hardly blame him, considering her condition. The prospect of losing him once more made her even more determined to dance again. She would, by God, and then she would go to him; whole and eager to please him. At least for a while.

And so, a little more than two years after the day of the accident, a triumphant Sara returned joyfully to the tango company and began to rehearse the new numbers for their next tour. She had not seen or heard from Efren for several months when a mutual friend told her about the tango workshop in Cancun and Efren's poem on the brochure. He would be there! "Perfect!", she said to herself. "I'll fly to Cancun and surprise him! I'll arrange to appear as a guest performer—he won't believe his eyes!" Her head spun with the plans she would have to make, and pictured the look on his face as she imagined the scene. The lights would dim, and out she would come in a sexy blue—no—red dress, as lithe and as fabulous as ever. He would be so proud of her, and so happy to see her. Her heart beat rapidly as she called the airline to secure her ticket.

At last, it was time to leave. She could scarcely conceal her excitement as she took a cab to the airport. It had rained earlier and now a full moon shone on the wet asphalt ahead of them as if to clear a path for her. And then, as she paid the cabby and took her bags to the ticket counter, she was told that her flight would be delayed until the next morning because of an unusual circumstance. A passenger had died suddenly during the last leg of the incoming flight. The plane made an emergency landing at an outlying airport, and the coroner had to be called. All passengers were being held while an investigation took place. Merde! "Is there any chance I can get another flight out tonight?" she asked the counter clerk. "So sorry miss, but there's nothing I can do. There are no other flights scheduled for Cancun until tomorrow morning." "Never mind," Sara said, as she turned in desperation from the young clerk and walked dejectedly toward the waiting area. To make matters worse, she collided with a buffoon of a man who came hurrying around the corner and watched in horror as he spun away from her, dropping his papers as he tottered and fell. She did what she could to help him gather his belongings, apologizing profusely. He barely acknowledged her efforts, struggled to raise his enormous girth to his feet, grabbed his papers and waddled off, huffing and red-faced. "Silly oaf" she said to herself, and turned to leave when she heard someone calling her name. Looking for the source, she saw a vaguely familiar man smiling and waving at her amid the scurrying people. Then she recognized him. It was Rudolfo, a classmate from her secondary school. It surprised her to see he was in a pilot's uniform, and looking quite dashing at that. Her mind racing, she greeted him and told him of her plight, asking for his advice and praying that he could offer a solution.

Now, unbeknownst to the two of them, the moon was in syzygy that night. This of all nights—the one night in every twelve years when the sun, the moon and the earth are in perfect alignment. The tides, the heavens, flora, fauna and all human affairs are affected in unpredictable and bizarre ways during a time of syzygy. Emotions abound, unexpected events mysteriously occur, and things on earth seem weirdly off-kilter.

The pair of old friends at the airport were about to be unwitting players in this celestial drama. Sara had a need, and amazingly, Rudolfo had the solution as he was about to begin a charter flight to, of all places, Cancun! He was flying solo to pick up a cargo awaiting his arrival. Blessing the fates for this gift of good fortune, they retrieved Sara's bags and set off for the tropics; Sara with renewed excitement at the prospect of seeing Efren again, and Rudolfo with a gleam in his eye at the prospect of having a few intimate hours in a small plane with the secret and unrequited love of his adolescent dreams; the ethereal Sara.

*   *   *

Figure Four

LA MORDITA
(The Little Bite)

As a man dances with a woman, there are times when he may wish to shake things up a bit and interrupt the reverie of their tango. After two or three Ochos (figure eights), and as her foot glides past him, he will set his foot right in front of hers, blocking it. As he feels the side of her foot against his, he steps toward her, placing his other foot next to hers in such a manner that her foot becomes sandwiched between his. Trapped thusly, she must wait patiently for his next move. He may remove one of his feet while guiding her over the other, or he may step back only to lunge forward again, helping himself to another "bite". He waits until he's good and ready to make his move, as he has all the power at this point. But the wise and intelligent tanguero will take his bites sparingly, because he knows that the sin of gluttony can cause him to over-play his hand (or, in this case, his foot), and in the eyes of the woman, make him look the fool.

As Galindo spun away from the young woman at the airport, he cursed under his breath. The people nearest him made way for this hulk of a man as he pirouetted past them along the floor tiles, barely missing several other people. They watched, astounded and amused as he turned on his heels, and then found his balance at the last moment, just short of losing his dignity in what might have been an enormous pratfall. Gathering himself together, he proceeded with haste to the check-in area. His name was Galindo Alfredo Galuppo, and he was on his way to "Tango In The Tropics" with Miriam, his wife of twenty-three years. He still considered her to be his beautiful bride, the love of his life—his treasure. She was the one person in the world who loved him for his intrinsic qualities: his adventurous spirit, his intellectual curiosity, his gourmet cooking and his incredible prowess and stamina during their frequent bouts of lovemaking. He could turn a lazy afternoon into hours of pleasure, and then cook up a four course gourmand's delight.

In truth, Galindo was a giant anomaly. He was a pork-pie of a man, eating his way through life; joyfully processing huge amounts of food in record time through his eager mouth. He could devour a half pound hamburger in a half dozen bites; a few chomps here and there, and down it would drop into his hollow gourd of a stomach. It was a real experience just to watch him eat. He became a legend at the restaurants he and Miriam frequented. Waiters and fellow diners alike were in awe of his capacity, and it was said they would bet on the number of steaks or desserts he would polish off on any given night.

How then, could such a man walk away from the table, delicately take his wife by the hand, perambulate in an ungainly manner to the dance floor, and then maneuver himself, gliding her elegantly around the crowded floor, as smooth as moonlight on the stillness of a quiet lake? Yet, he did, and he did it with aplomb, for Galindo was born with natural rhythm and coordination in spite of his size. And like many Argentineans, his obsession with the tango matched his insatiable culinary appetite. Of course, with Galindo, that was saying a lot. In fact, as far as he was concerned, the tango was the pinnacle of the art of dance. It stimulated his passions and challenged his intellect. To Galindo, the tango was to dancing like chess was to checkers. It was the thinking man's dance—*la ultima.*

He was the envy of his fellow tangueros, whose jealousy often got the best of them, and often when gliding past them on the dance floor, he could hear them muttering snide remarks, grouped in corners like a gaggle of gossipy girls. He would catch a word here and there: ". . . must be awfully horny . . ." ". . . how can he . . ." "wife put up with", etc. Then Galindo would glide by them, as smooth as cream custard, leaning forward a bit so that his heart was beating with Miriam's, a mutually divine smile on both their faces, cheeks touching, eyes almost closed. The music and rhythm infused their beings, and inspired Galindo to bring his legs and feet under the spell of his passionate soul. His envious contemporaries sighed as he danced by, knowing that dancing with Galindo became the pursuit of many a female, as the experience was a sensual one.

Galindo's devotion to Miriam, however, allowed him no more than one or two tangos with any one of this assortment of female temptresses before he would diplomatically decline their overtures, stating amiably "I'm sorry, but I've promised the next tango to my lovely wife." This display of husbandly duty and devotion brought him the admiration of some, and the rankle of others. It became a double edged sword, which caused him some difficulties in the past, which he would rather forget. But, he was used to controversy ever since child-hood, and he did his best to placate his critics with a jovial spirit and a modicum of humility

Galindo's father was a master chef from Italy who was brought to Argentina by a wealthy restaurateur. He was a large man himself, with the ruddy complexion and copper hair of many Northern Italians. And he was handsome enough to catch the eye of a buxom, beautiful Argentinean dancer who became his wife and then the proud mother of their chubby little cherub with rosy pink cheeks. His beautifully shaped head was tousled with golden blonde ringlets. They named him Galindo and doted on him shamelessly, captivated by his infectious laugh and mischievous blue eyes. As he grew older, he enjoyed accompanying his mom to the restaurant where his father reigned over his chefdom. His father's specialty was desserts, and the little Galindo's eyes would grow large as lumps of sweet pastry dough became delectable puffs infused with sumptuous fillings. These treats he later learned to use to his advantage when his classmates would torment him, eventually turning them into his very best friends.

Each day, Galindo would look forward to the end of the school day, when he could go to the restaurant. He was enamored of the copper pans, giving off the delicious smell of caramelized sugar, and he would watch entranced, as the sugar was poured out, skillfully transformed by his father into delicate amber threads, domed over a sumptuous *bombe*. Yes, little Galindo watched and tasted, and the images and lingual satisfactions became part and parcel of his waking hours and surfaced often in his dreams at night. Soon, little Galindo became large Galindo, and then larger and larger. As time passed, his interest in eating expanded into his interest in creating what he was eating. Thus, upon graduating from school, he apprenticed with his father and then was off to France to study at the French Culinary Institute where he excelled in his studies and immersed himself in the creating of unique and delectable dishes featuring a variety of exotic flora and fauna.

It was there in France that Galindo discovered his love for and mastery of the dance of his roots—his country—the Argentine tango. He loved the music, the movement, the way it made him feel. It transformed him into a suave, secure and sensual man, irresistible to women. The music would scarcely begin when his new persona would emerge and envelop him. This surprising phenomenon enlivened his evenings and his love life. As time passed, his élan with the dance along with his jovial manner made him a hit with the women, and it was through the tango that he met, courted and married Miriam, who was a British journalist, sent to France on an assignment to report on the surging popularity of the tango in postwar Paris. She was attracted to his bon-vivant manner and his charming, affable demeanor. The moment he held her for their first tango, she was his, as he was entirely and totally hers. He showered her with attention and roses and cooked her sumptuous meals. One night, after such a meal, he proffered to her a marriage proposal to which he simply would not take no for an answer. She happily accepted, and wasted no time arranging a simple but elegant wedding with many tango friends, celebrating the evening with them at "Los Martinets". Tango after tango followed, well into the evening which filled them with memories relived many years later.

They lived in a flat on the Rue de Marchet, and their days were spent as with most married couples, decorating their living space and then living and loving within those walls, which soon permeated with the delicious smells of Galindo's cooking assignments. Evenings were devoted to the tango dancing in little clubs and gathering around themselves a group of convivial dance mates. Then came graduation., and Galindo's culinary talents brought him the highest certification in his field as well as his first employment at one of Argentina's finest hotels. There he established his unrivaled reputation as the "gourmand's gourmet." As his circle of influence grew, he and Miriam continued their tryst with the tango, loving it fiercely, and as most tangueros do, dancing it nightly and into the dawn.

Ah, if life as they knew it could maintain its course, Galindo and Miriam would have lived sublimely, content in the world of their making. But soon, Galndo's buoyant spirit began to sag. His well-meaning friends suddenly seemed critical and sarcastic and in his mind, they were laughing behind his back. He began to think the women he danced with were patronizing him, thinking him to be a fat oaf. If that weren't bad enough, at night the sumptuous feasts which once filled his dreams were becoming nightmares.

In one recurring dream, he lay naked on a table, staring up at a blinding light. There were men in white coats looking down at him. Doctors, he supposed. He tried to move, but he couldn't—his arms were like lead. He opened his mouth to scream at them, but nothing came out. And then, he noticed the mirror above him. To his horror, his legs were separated from the trunk of his body, and like the trunk of a tree, his middle was sliced through as nice as you please. Surprisingly, there was no blood. The doctors probed and measured, notated and analyzed. He could hear, but could not respond. He found he could move his eyes, but only managed to roll them desperately to and fro, but without attracting an iota of attention. He strained desperately to hear what they were saying about his condition, but only managed to catch a few words here and there. "Look there", one of them said, "a—circle—mushroom soufle—age 10." "Yes", another said, "see—ring—milky core? Junior foods, one and a half". "Oh my God", Galindo cried, "they're counting the rings of fat and food through my middle and analyzing me like a tree to determine my age and how I died. I am dead! Fat and dead!"

Each night, the dream would end in the same manner. As he watched in horror, his legs would drop off the end of the table and run for the door. The doctors would say "Too bad, how sad.", as they began drawing a white sheet up and over what was left of him, covering his head which was turning frantically from side to side, his voice, recovered now, yelling "No! No! No!" Many mornings he would awaken, dripping rivulets of sweat, entangled in the bed sheets and struggling wildly as Miriam tried to comfort him. He was distraught, beaten, miserable with himself. But, again life turned in his favor and sent a message of salvation to Galindo Galluppo.

It was a cloudy afternoon in Buenos Aires when the invitation came. It was a beautifully designed brochure, red and yellow in color, oozing warmth and promising adventure. "Tango in the Tropics" it touted. As it happened, it was near the end of March in Argentina, which ushers in cooling winds, announcing the coming of fall and the passing of summer and warm balmy evenings. How tempting, Galindo thought. Tango in the Yucatan, the land of the Mayans. Languorous tropical breezes—white sand beaches and the gentle lapping of the caressing seas on my ankles. He could almost feel the sensation, and longed for it. It was just the incentive he needed to fuel his determination to lose the accursed pounds which were weighing heavily on his life. Three months until the workshop . . . 12 weeks.

He would casually mention the invitation to Miriam who he knew was always up for travel and the romance of a tango weekend. But he wouldn't mention his diet plan. He would rather surprise her. Besides, what if he should fail? To cinch the deal, he told her he would have an opportunity to bring back to Buenos Aires a rare tropical fruit virtually unknown in South America, but famous in the Yucatan for its delicate flavor and aphrodisiac qualities. The fruit was a relative of the Black Zapote, and it was found in only two places in the world: the jungles of India and the Yucatan. This exotic delicacy had intrigued him ever since he was told of it by Rudolfo, a friend who happened to be a pilot who flew many off-duty missions from Argentina to Mexico. To intrigue Galindo even more, Rudolfo spoke highly of its efficacy in increasing the libido with its delicate but pungent strands which revealed themselves when the dark red globe they inhabited was halved and opened. The tree on which the zapote grew, had low spreading branches that enabled the fruit to be easily harvested. If his memory served him well, the area in which it grew and was most prolific was but an hour or so walk from the site of the workshop. Though Galindo's job was secure, he felt his reputation was lagging. Introducing a delicacy like the Black Zapote to the culinary crowd in Buenos Aires would do a lot to get their attention once more.

With Miriam's eager assent, the deposit for their registration was sent to the workshop promoters, and arrangements were made to meet with Rudolfo at the airport prior to their departure. According to the plan, Galindo's job was to scout the exact location of the fruit and hire a crew of local pickers and packers. Rudolfo would wait at the airport on the Saturday of the workshop to fly the passion packed perishables back to Argentina, then to the hotel, where they would be placed in cold storage to await Galindo's return. A perfect plan. What could go wrong?

And now, the real challenge: Galindo was determined to lose twelve pounds a week. In twelve weeks, he would lose a hundred and forty four pounds! He set to the task just as he set out to become a chef—with discipline and determination. He replaced his desire for delicacies with snacks of yogurt, fruit, carrots and celery. He vanquished his taste for treats with tea and flatbread and his lust for liver and onions with lunges, leaps and jumping jacks. The resulting energy he put to use by increasing the duration and frequency of his amorous attention to Miriam, with an ardor that left her breathless.

And so, the weeks passed, and then the months, and twice they had to shop for new clothes for the diminishing Galindo. Miriam could scarcely believe her eyes. Oh, he was still portly and cuddly, and twice the size of a normal man of five foot five, but after losing a hundred and twenty pounds, he was now only twice the width of his height.

At last, the time came for packing and the harrowing trip to the airport through the hazy, smoggy, clogged streets of the city. After unloading their bags and getting Miriam into one of the long lines to hold their place for ticketing, Galindo bussed her on the cheek and proceeded to rush to his meeting with Rudolfo to complete the plan.

It was in his haste as he ran down the corridor that he turned the corner and careened off the beautiful girl who tried to say something to him. But being embarrassed and completely off balance, he ignored her and proceeded to the café` where Rudolfo sat waiting.

"Hola, Rudolfo, mi amigo . . . que tal?" Galindo's query was answered by the ever-charming pilot. *"Hola, Galindo. Como va?"* Rudolfo enjoyed Galindo for his cavalier attitude, and the unique assignment he spoke of interested him particularly. Especially because it would offer him an opportunity to take Sara to the Yucatan to meet her so-called lover. Even though the thought of facilitating their reunion annoyed him, the prospect of spending several hours with her in the cockpit of his plane would give him a window of time to work his magic on her. Who could tell? One never knows what could transpire on such a cozy flight, Rudolfo mused as he greeted Galindo and tried to get his mind on the assignment. "We'll meet tomorrow at the hotel on Isla Flores, and I'll go over the arrangements with the pickers and introduce you to my contact for the trucks. Everything has to work like clockwork, my friend. The fruit will be ready to take on Saturday by noon. I'm sure you won't mind a day or two in the tropics, eh?" Not likely, thought Rudolfo. He grinned as he agreed to all the details, and a mutually satisfactory fee was arranged. Whereupon Rudolfo flashed his dazzling smile as he held his hand out to seal their negotiations and bid Galindo "adios".

Their arrangements having been made to Galindo's satisfaction, he rejoined Miriam just as she arrived at the airline counter. The jovial clerk smiled as she assigned their seats and wished them a pleasurable trip. "You watch yourselves over there on Isla Flores," she said with a wink. "There's going to be a full moon, and I understand a very special one. It could be very romantic!" Galindo smiled and took Miriam's arm as they made their way to the waiting area. They surveyed their fellow passengers, and thought they recognized one of the fellows from the local tango scene. "Isn't that Efren?" He asked Miriam, but they boarded ahead of him, and they lost sight of him before she had a chance to reply.

At last they were boarded and settled in first class, which they found was worth the price, as two seats in coach were necessary for accommodating Galindo's ample frame. It was the first time they could really relax since climbing into the taxi back home. Miriam could tell that Galindo had something on his mind, and had a suspicion it had to do with his meeting with Rudolfo. "What are you thinking, amor?" "Nothing, nothing . . . please don't worry, it's not important." But Miriam persisted, and he finally admitted to having second thoughts about the whole scheme. "Supposing it should rain? It rains all the time in the jungle. Supposing the pickers are incompetent? Worse yet, what if the Zapote fruit is over-ripe, or in scarce supply? I'm beginning to think this was a big mistake." But, Miriam soothed and reassured him, as she always did, and he knew she would. "Please, Galindo. You worry too much. Everything will be fine." But as the words came out of her mouth, there was a sudden drop in cabin pressure—enough to startle even the most jaded air travelers.

"Ladies and gentlemen," the stewardess addressed them. "Please don't be alarmed. We've reached our cruising altitude, and the Captain has asked that you remain seated with your seatbelts in the locked position until further notice. We're experiencing unusual turbulence, but he assures us it won't last long. I'll be bringing you your drinks and snacks soon, and until then, please take the time to read the safety instructions again, just as a precaution." She then hastened to her jumpseat and buckled up.

When two people have been married as long as Galindo and Miriam had, it was common knowledge that they could read each other's thoughts. In an instant, they both thought of the smiling clerk at the airline counter and her mention of some "celestial hijinks" which were about to occur. But, they reasoned, surely a heavenly disruption of that magnitude would have made its way into the news, and they had neither heard nor read any such stories. So, they leaned back, slept a bit and finally ate. There were a few more unsettling ups and downs as they passed over mountainous peaks, already dusted with snow. They crossed over the highest peaks, and watched in awe as they glistened back at them in icy grandeur. They assured themselves that the worst was over, happy to be in the silver cocoon high above the cold landscape, and they slept again, and dreamed dreams of big, round moons traveling across skies pulsing with undulating clouds and mysterious creatures dressed in garments of starry silk.

"Ladies and gentlemen, thank you for your patience," the pert attendant chirped. They awoke groggy but happy to be informed they were about to descend in short order. Just enough time to freshen up and clear their heads. Happy to be disembarking at last, they gathered up their belongings and waited for what seemed forever to catch their first glimpse of paradise. Happily, they weren't disappointed as the first soothing Caribbean breeze enveloped them; warm and sultry and welcoming. They joined the other passengers headed for the ferry dock where they would embark on the little boat that would carry them to Isla Flores and the Rey Caribe Resort. Galindo glanced at the bright blue morning sky, matched in brilliance by the azure water, and sighed deeply. In spite of his promise to Miriam to relax, he couldn't help giving a perfunctory search of the island's green interior for a glimpse of his precious Zapote trees. His visual quest was interrupted by the sound of the ferry's engine throttling down and the bump of the boat against the dock.

They followed the others up the gravel path, and as they reached the top, the El Rey Caribe stood before them, grand and glorious, calling them into its shady lobby. No doors stood between them and the beautiful slate floor that led to the registration desk. There were potted palms everywhere, and one could not tell where the outdoors ended and the indoors began. Exotic orchids encroached their way into the lobby, finding a space to grow in every nook and cranny of the room. Uncommonly large flowers were bundled and arranged in their vases like bright islands of fragrant color on the golden warmth of the polished teak tables. The parade of pilgrims to paradise shuffled in across the slate floor, lining up to be granted access to their awaiting bungalows. Rooms were assigned, and Galindo and Miriam followed the tanned and smiling bellboy to Number 22, situated conveniently on the path closest to the restaurant. They paid the boy, and as they unpacked they planned their afternoon.

The most pressing order of business for Galindo was to contact the guides and pickers who were recommended to him by the concierge for the Saturday morning harvest. *"Amor,"* said Galindo to Miriam, after several phone calls to the desk, "It's all arranged. It couldn't have been easier, and I'm meeting with them right now in the lobby. But, I'm starving, and when I get back, I should have a little snack. Can we do that, *mi vida?"*

And so, Galindo left Miriam to finish the unpacking and headed for the reception area. Of course, when things seem to go as planned, you can be sure there will always be the unexpected, especially when the cosmos is playing tricks as it was in that time of syzygy—especially in the languid tropics in the afternoon. But, for now, Galindo was pleased with his progress, blessed his luck and chose to ignore that little inkle of doubt the crept into his thoughts. Had he listened, the inkle would have revealed to him that the boys were cousins of the concierge; and the sons of his father's brother who was a bit lacking in the ways of good business. In fact, their father was the island philanderer, and never knew when to stop drinking the pulque, which was bound to affect his judgment when he had to meet someone at 5 a.m. in the jungles of Isla Flores.

Galindo's appetite over-rode his uneasiness as he retrieved Miriam and filled her in on his business arrangement as they headed for the café for Galindo's second lunch, (which was supposed to be a light snack, as he didn't want to eat too much before dinner.) Miriam sighed as he consumed an enormous "American Hamburger," and wolfed down an order of fries, followed by a lovely caramel cream delight. She knew his brief bout of calorie cutting would be followed by a binge of belt loosening, but rather than nag, she smiled and took his arm as they left for a little nap. As it turned out, they slept through dinner, exhausted from their trip, as did many of the participants. Just as well, for the next two days and nights would test their mettle.

*   *   *

"Hola, amigas!" the rotund man and his wife greeted us as we met on the path outside the café after breakfast. "We're Galindo and Miriam from Buenos Aires. We saw you on the ferry, remember? Why don't you join us?" We had noticed them on the boat (who wouldn't?), and were happy to see someone familiar. "Love to! This is Dixie and Dawn, and I'm Marie. We're from California, and we're really looking forward to this morning's class." After a few more verbal exchanges, we crossed the vast expanse of lawn together, and wound our way along the promenade. The girls and I walked ahead of the puffing Galindo and his wife, up the stairs to the veranda and through the French doors which led into the large ballroom. We were barely inside, when all eyes turned in our direction, not because of us, but because of the sound of the door banging against the wall and the sight of the enormous man sandwiched between the door and the wall so that his lady could enter. Those who knew Galindo were not surprised; in fact they thought he looked a bit slimmer than they remembered. Those who didn't know him were amazed. "He's going to take class?" one of the women asked in hushed tones. Her friend chimed in "He's not dancing with me." Of course when they saw him in action, they would be using all their wiles to have their turn with him on the dance floor. In the meantime, Miriam and Galindo managed to collect themselves and find a space by the three of us.

I sat back observing the scene around me. Some students were sitting on the floor in groups, while others were scattered around the room, chatting with friends. I wondered who would become my friends—my enemies—or just a pain in the rear. Would I find a good tango partner among them, and who might it be best to avoid? Everyone eyed each other, futilely trying to read behind the masks we all wore. A youngish man and his friend came over and introduced themselves to us as Tony and Carlos. I liked Carlos right away.

Quiet and unassuming he was, nice and harmless. Was I attracted to him, or just wanting to play it safe? Then a tall man in a black shirt and black linen pants caught my eye. I hadn't met him before, and made a mental note to do just that. Some scantily clad girls were warming up, showing off their tango technique as well as their other attributes—as usual. I rose from my seat, using the excuse of warming up to get closer to mister black shirt, when I glanced up at the observation windows which flanked the upstairs hallway that ran the length of the balcony. From above, one could watch the activity below from a good vantage point without being noticed. Except that I did notice. There above the room, framed in the window was a face I would not soon forget. Its expression was pinched; tense and grim. It was a face of white-skinned desperation, with eyes like two lasers staring out starkly above the nostrils, which flared out over a slash of a mouth. A face enshrouded in a helmet of red hair with straight bangs which sliced themselves across a taut forehead, cornered neatly at the temples and continued down to end at both sides of a jutting jaw like a couple of commas. "Who on earth is that miserable soul?" I asked myself. My musings and apprehensions grew as she abruptly left her vantage point, and disappeared. Then, the attention in the room shifted to the curved stairway leading to the balcony. The specter of her face reappeared and all conversation and movement in the room ceased. This must be Margo, the name on my flyer which followed "produced and coordinated by". She was followed by the teaching staff, and all hearts quickened as their eagerly awaited maestros and their partners descended down to their waiting minions, led by the legendary "dragon" lady" herself. It was going to be quite a weekend!

*   *   *

Figure Five

EL GANCHO
(The Hook)

The tango is fraught with conflict. A man asks a woman to dance. He risks her rejection. He takes her in his arms but in his insecurity, he may grasp her hand so tightly that she will resist. Not wanting to be rude or to be thought "difficult", she continues to dance, though she grows weary of his impertinence. As she contemplates her dilemma, she is turned to the side and away from him as though being cast off. Then, she is pulled back whereupon she is in position to flick her foot backward, in close proximity to a very sensitive part of his anatomy. Another risk on his part. Not to be outdone, he retaliates with a flick of his own. They fascinate and excite their audience with ever increasing speed and passion; flashes of feet darting here and there—until they are spent and they surrender to the resolution of the music by finishing their dance. "El Gancho" is the lifeblood of el tango. It is the universal hook which baits its victims with promises of power, of position, of authority and notoriety among the maestros; and the seductive offer of romance and reckless abandon among the students. Some are just greedier than others.

I watched, fascinated, as Margo surveyed the room. It seemed this was the part of the workshop that she liked best. She was in charge, and she let everyone know it. She was one of those women who just couldn't leave life alone. She was always poking at it—demanding from it—a greedy little thing. I felt the brush of an arm against mine, and looked at the tall, slim figure next to me—Mr. black shirt. "Ah, Margo seems in top fighting form this morning, as usual," he said. "If you don't already know it, it's best not to cross her." He introduced himself to me as Ricardo.

Dixie and Dawn gave me that "knowing" look as I introduced them and myself. Just then, the murmur of our voices caught the attention of Margo. "Well, well, well!" she said, all but hissing. "Dixie and Dawn, I believe. How very nice to see you again. Who's your lovely friend?" She tried to be aloof and above us all, but the twitch in her eyes gave her away as I was introduced. Oh boy, I thought. The fireworks begin.

Evidently, there were more stories than people in that room, and the potential hooked me with its intrigue. I determined to satisfy my curiosity about as many of them as possible. The teachers themselves were a fascinating lot. As they were introduced, I recalled the many stories and rumors I had heard about them.

Standing to the right of Margo was the young and handsome Armando, with his curly dark hair and his mestizo swarthiness. Armando, who had captured,(then broken), Dawn's heart while she was on a tango trip to Buenos Aires. I watched her carefully while he was introduced, hoping she wouldn't be inclined to backslide into his arms again. Not that I could blame her, as he exuded sensuality. No doubt their previous relationship was the cause of Margo's guile toward Dawn. She glanced our way as she placed her hand on the ripple of muscle on his arm in a proprietary manner. He was her baby, and there would be no doubt about it. I could smell the tension between them as his partner came forward, introduced as Rosa. Round-cheeked and round-busted she was, with the most unusual eyes. They were almost black, with coal black rims—deep and foreboding, yet inviting you in for a visit. Margo would have trouble keeping her own eyes on that one.

Claudio and Patricia joined Armando and Rosa as their names were called, greeting everyone with genuine charm. One of the few happily married couples in the tango world, they were valuable teachers, known for their excellent command of the basic fundamentals of the dance. They were wonderful to watch while they danced, with their clean, classic moves and original dance stylings. They traveled twice a year to Spain, looking for anything new and different in the dance, or tango music which served to keep them up to date in spite of their age. They visited friends and relatives, and connected with the Flamenco crowd, enjoying the ferias, while dancing and singing until dawn. The rumor was that a few years ago, Margo followed them, imposing on their good will and finagling a place to stay. They did their best to entertain her and introduced her to several young bachelors. However, within several days it came back to them from various sources that she had bedded them all. The worst of it was that she fell madly in love with one young man who was the brother of their friend Romero. Young he was, all right . . . fifteen, and quite randy. He, of course, enjoyed the admiration he received from his peers for taking on an "older woman". In order to get Margo out of the country, (by request from the boy's family) they cut their visit short and accompanied her back to the States. The Spaniards breathed a sigh of relief, and neither Claudio nor Patricia mentioned it again.

And now, my favorite couple came forward. I had seen them in a fabulous tango show in L.A., and dreamed tango dreams for many nights afterward. They influenced my pursuit of the dance, and I tried to copy Graciela's style for months. I think I got it, a little. They weren't married, but had been living and dancing together for at least ten years. Steady and dependable, but with lots of fire and passion in their dancing, they would grace our weekend with their inimitable style. I hoped the stories of trouble from an incident in San Francisco would not alter their love for each other, though I knew of Gabriel's volatile temper and healthy libido. As they stepped in line with the others, Margo looked anxiously in the direction of the door. There was one maestro missing—Aldo. He was one of the big draws of the weekend. It would be really disappointing if he didn't show up. But Margo continued with her itinerary and gave us the details regarding the schedule of classes, and who would be teaching what.

If the idea that Senor Aldo might not show up was disappointing to me, even more so was the fact that there was also no sign of Efren. I began to wonder if I had been mistaken in reading in the brochure that he was attending. I would have to check it later. We were asked to form groups according to the classes we wanted to take. There would only to be two today, so I opted for Valse Cruzada with Aldo. I spied Ricardo standing with the "Valse" guys, and that settled it. Also, I wanted to get a chance to observe Aldo in action.

As we filed into class, I noticed Dawn in a group of students that would learn the intricacies of special embellishments that would add to the interest of the tango. The class was taught by Armando and Rosa. "No, no!" I wanted to shout and stop her from making a big mistake in taking up with Armando again. I was worried for my friend, not just because of Margo, but I had heard that he had a wife and baby living in the outskirts of Buenos Aires, to say nothing of the girl he left behind after teaching for a weekend in San Francisco. "Well," I told myself. "Stay out of it. Dawn's a big girl. She can handle it . . . you take care of yourself." I decided to take my own advice and entered the class just as Aldo asked everyone to introduce themselves, and take a partner. I happily paired up with Ricardo, jumping in front of Lucy and her blonde braids before she knew what hit her.

It was well known and widely circulated that tango maestros tended to be temperamental and highly emotional, and Aldo was no exception. In his time, Aldo Romero was known as "El Gato" for his sinewy, cat-like technique with the tango. His parents had settled in Argentina from Venezuela during the Peron regime, which was the heyday of tango parties and milongas. Tango had become a popular diversion for many of the wealthy American socialites who were hooked by its heady lure. They came to Argentina in droves, and groveled at the feet of the handsome and famous tangueros. Like many of his tango compatriats, Aldo had a way with the ladies. He was also the catalyst that kept the others going, promoting the tango by putting on spectacular, seductive tango shows, and giving them his advice on how to keep the American ladies happy and spending money. He unified the teachers and defined the tango scene for them. They were all envious of his smooth and elegant style, as all the men were today. He was a slim, handsome "Astaire-like" figure of a man, with all the Latin charm and romantic appetite of a Valentino. He had affairs, got married, fathered children, had more affairs, and enchanted eager women from sea to sea with his savoir-faire and impeccable manner. And now, here he was, ready to impart to us all that style and charm.

He had barely begun to demonstrate the first step of the Tango Waltz when the first of many tango "incidents" intruded on our weekend. There was an interesting canard circulating that Aldo had an aversion to being touched by the students in class. It was part of his mystique, and in truth, he was the only maestro who didn't use a partner, or at least one of the students to demonstrate the women's steps. This common knowledge somehow missed the ears of "Lucy with the braids". I had taken Ricardo from her, so when Aldo came around to see that we fledglings were dancing properly, Lucy thought she would throw her charms at Aldo and have herself a good partner. Now, Lucy was young, very pretty, and quite well-endowed, however that was not enough to overcome Aldo's initial reaction. As Lucy stepped forward, asking for help with the step, she threw her arms around his neck, whereupon Aldo quickly stepped back, thrust her hands down with both of his and reprimanded her in front of all of us. Lucy, embarrassed and angry, retorted in equal volume, "You know what, Senor? I paid a lot of money to learn that step, and I expect you to teach it to me." All motion in the class ceased, and we watched, fascinated as her tirade continued. "If you're too damn touchy to do that, don't be surprised if I have a talk with Margo about your silly little fetish." Taken aback, but not down for the count, he calmed her with his ubiquitous smile. "I'm so sorry if I caused you any discomfort, my lovely girl. It's just a silly reaction I had. If you'll allow me, rather than in class, I'll be glad to help you later." Of course we all knew where that was going—straight to the sack. Class resumed, but there was a lighter atmosphere in the room, and everyone was secretly grinning, delighted with another tango tale to tell.

At last, it was time for our lunch break. I decided to skip the meal, and I headed for the bungalow. I passed groups of people sunning or snacking on the lawn as I sauntered down the path. It was a beautiful day, a beautiful place, and I had already learned a lot and wanted more. My energy was low from the morning's activities and I looked forward to a bit of time to myself. I arrived at the bungalow, checked for messages (there were none), splashed cool water on my face, tidied up my hair and fought the urge to lie down on the bed. I knew better than to tempt the sleepy state I was in, and had a protein bar and bottle of water instead. As I ate, I checked the brochure I received in the mail and sure enough, it said "We are pleased to announce that Sr. Montoya will be in attendance." "Well, maybe he was just detained, and will show up later, I said to myself." I checked my image in the mirror and headed back to the ballroom for the afternoon class. It was to be on the figure named "La Cadena", one of the most complicated and difficult of all the moves.

The afternoon class and that night's milonga were a blur as I climbed exhausted into bed. My mind needed a break from the stimulation, physical workout and drama that had already occurred. I sank into the soft recesses of my thoughts, barely aware of the animated chatter between Dixie and Dawn. Fortunately, I had no idea that the chain of events that tomorrow would bring would far exceed those that had hooked me today. But, where was Efren?

*　　*　　*

Figure Six

LA CADENA
(The Chain)

There are many types of chains; daisy chains and chains of command. Chains that bind can be troublesome, as they may cause chain reactions. The tango chain is a very tricky figure that is rarely done, as it's not widely known, and only executed by the most advanced dancers. It's interesting to watch, because it begins imperceptibly, and then gradually accelerates, taking on a life of its own. At first glance, it's the man who begins the momentum by turning the woman to his left, inserting his right foot between her feet, which signals her to do the same while turning around him to her right. He turns again without a pause, inserting his foot and she reciprocates again, so that on and on they go, circling round and round like tango dervishes, which on a crowded dance floor can become a vicious circle.

The day that brought the tango seekers to Isla Flores was the same day that the little chartered plane lifted off the tarmac, and headed in the same direction. While Galindo, Miriam and the three girls from L.A. were enjoying their ferry ride to the Rey Caribe, high and away above the clouds, Rudolfo was intent upon impressing Sara with his aeronautical expertise. Truth be told, he was consumed with seducing her.

They were skirting the highest volcano on earth, on the Chilean side of the Andes, known as Ojos del Salado; "The Crying Eyes." He began telling her of the region's mountainous and rugged terrain, and the narrow coastline to the west with its precipitous cliffs overhanging the roiling sea. As they banked toward that area of the Pacific, he embellished his narrative with the legend of how many a sailor had perished on its shores. He had her attention now, and casually reached across her, while pointing in the direction of one of the snow covered peaks, drawing closer to his quarry. The scent of her excited him, and in his ardor he grew careless and failed to notice the OAT reading on the instrument panel, which was indicating that the outside temperature had dropped to a dangerous low—in fact, it was at that moment low enough to ice the wings of the small plane. Before realizing their predicament, the oxygen system froze, so that the two occupants of the land-bound missile became disoriented and were blessedly unaware of their impending doom. They never saw the inky blackness of the coastline waters or, rising up from its edge, the stark whiteness of the snow covered cliff, which came rushing up to meet them.

*　　*　　*

The following morning, slivers of sunlight found their way through the shutters in Rosa's bungalow. Armando blinked as, like a laser, the light sliced its way through his eyelids, ending the fitful sleep into which he fell after he and Rosa made love. He quietly turned form her sleeping figure and slipped out of the bed noiselessly, going to the window to breathe in the cool dawn air. He opened the blinds a bit to clear his head and stood transfixed as the sun began to darken. For a minute, he thought he was still dreaming, and he closed his eyes and opened them again to clear the sleep away. Then it hit him. A solar eclipse! He remembered reading about it before leaving Argentina. The moon would advance until the sun surrendered its warmth and light to the black orb, leaving but a slim glowing halo for the earth to position itself upon. It was beautiful, but he was careful to watch through a tiny hole made by his fists. His grandfather taught him how to see the halo without harming his eyes during the last eclipse. Armando figured it to be around 1973, and his grandfather called it a syzygy, a strange and magical sounding word to a small boy. He remembered looking it up in the dictionary that afternoon, and repeating it over and over . . . syzygy, syzygy. It happened when the sun, moon and earth found themselves in perfect alignment. It was legend in Argentina, that during a syzygy, the cows would all go home, and even the ants disappeared. The sky turns dark blue, inviting the stars to show themselves again. The tides answer the call of the moon and exceed their normal boundaries, and all humanity becomes restless and senselessly agitated.

Armando felt that restlessness, and gazed at the indigo sky where the sun was now completely obscured. Set into the heavens were four bright planets lined up like lights on a runway heading toward the moon. He didn't remember hearing about anything like that before, and he felt a strangeness in the air. It was as though the darkness held a pinpoint of light directing him to peer deeply into his soul. Armando was not a religious man, but he could not escape the message; his moral ambiguity had imprisoned him; and his conquests had become his jailers.

He let his hands drop to his side, and stared at the sleeping figure of Rosa. Why did she keep him from leaving her? Did he have a conscience after all? And he was beholden to Margo—more than he would have liked. The woman in San Francisco—his wife in Argentina . . . even his mother! How could he let himself be tied in knots by these women? The more he tried to make sense of it all, the more frustrated he became. A minute ago, he thought he knew the answers, and now . . . Just then, Rosa began to stir. He didn't want a confrontation, not just now. He dressed quickly so that he could leave and think more clearly. But she was awake now, and sat up, staring at him in confusion. "Armando, why are you getting dressed . . . it's the middle of the night. Come back to bed!" "I can't, Rosa. I have to go. I can't explain now." But she grabbed the hand and held it tightly. "Amor, don't leave. Where are you going? What about the class? We have to teach!" But he shook her loose, grabbed his valise and left, hearing her cries as he closed the door.

*　　*　　*

Not twenty yards away in Bungalow 23, Dixie and Dawn, having slept through the eclipse, awoke to the sound of a light rain falling on the rooftop. It was now eight a.m., and still dark enough to cause them to murmur quietly, so as not to awaken their room-mate. "It seems so early, but I'm starved!" Dixie said in hushed tones. Dawn peered sleepily at the bedside clock, glowing in the half-darkened room. "Oh, my God! We've overslept! Why is it so dark?" They went to the shuttered windows, left partially open the night before, and peered into the misty garden. The giant leaves of the elephant plants hung heavily with the steamy accumulation of moisture. Though the rain had ceased and the clouds had cleared, the dimly lit sky belied the hour. The girls decided to dress and go to breakfast, and see if anyone at the café knew anything of the morning's mysterious events. They left Marie sleeping peacefully in the other room as they left, figuring she would need her sleep, as they had spent half the night gossiping and hashing out the possible explanations for Efren's absence. In addition, she had consumed quite a bit of wine. As for them, a good shot of expresso was in order, along with some food to clear their heads.

Entering the café, their eyes scanned the room and spotted Galindo and Miriam at a table by the buffet. As they approached, Galindo rose to greet them, but he'd not backed his chair out sufficiently, so as he came up, his thighs caught the edge of the table. The sudden upward motion tilted it, sending the sugar jar and various plates sliding across the top and coming to rest precariously close to the edge, just short of giving Miriam a lapful. The girls barely held their laughter, as Galindo composed himself and invited them to join their party. They gladly accepted and asked him if he and Miriam were going to the review that morning. "No, no, I can't" he replied. "Why don't the two of you have breakfast, and go to class with Miriam. You have a little time yet and I have some business to do." "What kind of business would you have out here?" they inquired. Flattered by their interest, he responded. "Have you heard of the Black Zapote?" The girls shook their heads, and encouraged him to go on. "Well" he said, casually examining his nails, "The Zapote is an exotic fruit which grows on a beautiful tree found only in the jungles around this part of the world. It has to be picked at the precise peak of ripeness to release it's deliciously sweet savor. I've hired some native pickers who are working as we speak, and I've chartered a plane to fly them back to Argentina where I will make the most superb and evocative desserts from them." The girls responded in amazement at having a chef in their midst, and begged for more information, but Galindo declined, as he was becoming concerned about finding his way to the harvesting through the dampened jungle. "I will bring you a sample", he promised, "but now I must excuse myself to make an important phone call. Timing is everything with these highly perishable fruits. I need to call the airport to check on my pilot's progress." He raised his considerable bulk to leave, and as a precaution, the three of them grabbed hold of the table in unison. Smiling good-naturedly, Galindo bussed his wife on the cheek, bid the girls goodbye, and left them to a hastily eaten repast.

*   *   *

I awakened from a deep sleep to the frantic buzzing of some sort of insect which seemed to be trapped within the slats of the shutters over my bed. I felt fuzzy-headed as I managed to free the frightened creature and shooed him back to the garden. The clock glowed in the darkened room: 11:11 a.m. "Damn!" I muttered to no one. "I missed the morning class. I forced myself out of bed and stumbled into the bathroom where a cold shower did its work. Just as I was adjusting the straps on my favorite dancing shoes, in came Dixie and Dawn, faces flushed and talking in rapid succession: "Marie, did you hear about the eclipse?" "We brought you some food!" "Eat fast—the afternoon class promises to be a blast. Everyone's up tight." "Oh yeah . . . Efren asked about you!"

* * *

Efren felt miserable. Exhausted and stressed out, he went to his bungalow as soon as he left the ballroom, and fell deeply asleep. His dreaming began softly, bringing the beckoning image of Sara to him, and then she turned away, still looking at him longingly as she began to leave. He saw himself in the dream, and he called out to her, but no sound came, and Sara kept walking, fading into the distance, until all he could see of her was her beautiful smile in a hazy fog. Then, suddenly he was on a tall mountain, in a strange and unfamiliar landscape on an icy field white with snow. Beneath the cliff's icy edge swirled black and ominous waters. Above him, the heavens were alive with whirling stars—more than he had ever seen, leaping and diving around a swollen gourd of a moon. He heard a sound behind him, and as he turned, an old tango song was heard, drawing him to its strains like a mythological siren. He had walked only a few steps, when he noticed that though there was new-fallen snow, his feet made no footprints. He was mesmerized by the phenomenon when a form materialized before him . . . a familiar form. It was the graceful shape of a woman with a hauntingly beautiful face. As he drew nearer to see her better, he realized the woman was dancing the tango . . . dancing in the snow. Her footpath, unlike Efren's, made deep gouges in the soft powder. She was executing a Cruzada, and the traces of her footfall were like a map leading to . . . where? Fascinated and curious, he followed her steps and let himself get so close as to see the tears streaming down her face. And then, just as the recognition hit him, the form and face of his beautiful Sara sank down into the snow. Horrified, he ran to save her, but the snow was falling in around her like a cascade of glistening white quicksand, until all that was left was a dimple in the snow where her beauty once stood. He fell to his knees and tried to dig her free, but to no avail. As he stood, bereft and crying, he looked this way and that as if she would appear again out of nowhere, but she didn't. He looked at the tracks her feet had made, and saw the clear figure of a cross in the snow. La Cruzada!

The horror of the dream awakened him, awash in dread and sorrow. The sweat-soaked sheets clung to him like a shroud and he was sickened from the intensity of it. Why had he left her in Argentina? He could have insisted that she come with him, or not have come at all. But of course, he could curse himself and the fates for all he was worth, but it changed nothing. He was here and she wasn't, and being the pragmatic person he was, he would finish his obligation to Margo, and when he returned to Argentina . . . well then, he would see how he felt. The onus of the dream was already lifting, and his thoughts of Sara were put back on the shelf. He glanced at the clock. 11 a.m. Just enough time to shower and shave, get some food, and be ready for the afternoon class. He donned his new black dockers, took his favorite shirt out of the suitcase, and slapped his cheeks with Boss, hoping to attract attention with the dash of his scent and the flash of his color. Maybe the American woman would be there and who knows what tonight might bring?

*　　*　　*

As the three of us closed the bungalow door, we heard a familiar voice coming from across the path. There on a garden bench sat Rosa, dabbing her red eyes, trying to catch her breath between sobs. I thought I had heard that sound coming from the bungalow next door as I was getting dressed earlier, but it was so faint, I thought I was mistaken. But now, the mystery was solved, and our sympathies were with Rosa as she blurted out her tale of woe. Why she stayed with Armando was beyond us, but there is a saying in Argentina: "The heart wants what the heart wants." So we commiserated with her, and tried to give her some good advice, though we were in a hurry so as not to miss class. First of all, she had to get some *cajones*, we told her, and stand up to him. Then, she had to play hard to get and not be such a pushover for his philandering and moody behavior. (I was a great one to talk. I got weak in the knees just thinking about Efren.) But, we put on a good front, gave her one of Dixie's "magic towelettes" to freshen her face, loaned her some lipstick and a comb, and up the path the four of us went, headed for another drama in "tango-land."

When we entered the now familiar ballroom, we spied Armando, as he looked up to see Rosa walking toward him, her head held high. They were to teach some tango embellishments - those extra moves the dancers make with their feet to give variety and excitement to the dance. However, since Rosa hadn't shown up, Margo took the opportunity to take her place, and she and Armando were in the middle of demonstrating a particularly clever gancho. As Rosa approached the couple, Margo cursed under her breath, and held on tighter to Armando, attempting to turn him away. Dixie gave Rosa a little nudge, and whispered "Go on, now. If you want him, take him." Resolutely, Rosa approached the two of them, and said "I'm here now, and I'm ready to take over with my partner." Now all of us were gleefully glued to the scene. Margo tried to ignore her and continued the figure, trying to keep Armando attached. Whereupon Rosa, now emboldened, grabbed her shoulder and spun her around to face her. "I said I am here to teach. You're not even doing the step right!" By this time, Margo had enough to swallow in front of the class, and wound up to whack Rosa on the cheek, but Rosa ducked, and as Margo's momentum carried her around, Rosa put a well-placed tango shoe to her rear, sending her sprawling. The class was applauding as Rosa turned and headed for the door, causing Armando, who was surprised and aroused by her "moxie", to follow her out.

Margo, contrary to what we thought she would do, sat up and started laughing! "My God, what got into that little wimp? Well, why are all of you standing there, staring? Help me up!" I was the closest to the action, so it fell to me to give her a hand, and then, who should step up to help me but Efren? I hadn't noticed him in all the excitement, but there he was, smiling his jowly smile. "Hola, little one," he said to me as we brought Margo to her feet. "I missed you this morning." Margo thanked us, and asked Efren to play some tangos so the class could practice for the dance that night. Then she went back to her office, and we didn't see her again until the next evening.

As for me, the rest of the day and that heavenly night were a blur. Efren and I danced and talked all afternoon, and in the evening, we had dinner together, skipped the milonga and walked along the beach by the ferry landing. We talked about the tango scene in L.A., and he told me I should come down to Argentina where I could really experience the soul of the Tango. We took off our shoes and sat on the sand and talked about his job and my job, and watched the wavelets lapping at our toes. We looked up at the stars, and saw the strange light that came down from the sky and fell on the water. Though there was to be a full moon that night, it was absent from above, but appeared to be shining from underneath the sea. The eeriness of it unnerved me a bit, but he stroked my hair and told me not to worry, and then he kissed me, long and hard.

*　　*　　*

Figure Seven

LOS ENCUENTROS
(The Encounters)

Experience is what you get when you don't get what you want. Nobody goes looking for the bad stuff, and the good stuff—well, although it brings many blessings when it occurs, it's quickly gone. Encounters with people can offer us the richest, though most unpredictable life experiences. Dancing the tango accelerates these experiences, good and bad. A well-known teacher in Brazil told me that the tango is the most highly emotional form of dancing because it deals with our basic chakras: the heart, the stomach and the bowels. It brings out our primitive passions. It has an answer for everyone, but to discover the answer, you must dance the tango with the right question in mind. The man's question lies within his deepest needs, and is limited by his perception of himself. The woman responds by her willingness to be led, not by the man, but through him. The terms of their encounter are mutual; their silence speaks volumes as they dance, heart to heart.

Saturday morning broke wetter than usual, and the path was still moist and slippery as Galindo trod it carefully, finally reaching the cafe for an early breakfast. He was anxious to get on with his day so that he could get back to ready himself for the "Noche del

Fandango"— the last night of the workshop. He left Miriam and the girls planning a ferry trip to Cancun for some serious shopping for the evening festivities, excusing himself to "take care of business".

He ate heartily, and left for the lobby to pick up the car he had reserved the previous day. Following the manager's directions, he drove to the area where the pickers had harvested the Zapotes, as he would need to examine the boxes for transport, making sure they were sufficiently buffered for the trip. His phone call to the airport on Thursday afternoon assured him that the pilot had filed his flight plan, and had taken off on schedule. There was no shortage of parking in the lot at the foot of the trail, being early in the day. The tourists would fill the lot later, coming from the Rey Caribe, as well as on tour buses that brought them from the Cancun ferry to see the ancient cenote, known as the "sacred well" that lay at the foot of the falls. Thousands of years ago, virgins were sacrificed at the cenote to assuage the rain god Chaak in periods of drought. Unaware of the significance of the site, Galindo nosed the little sedan into a shady spot, and thought it wise to leave his wallet on the seat before locking the door. His shorts had no pockets, nor did his t-shirt, so he attached the car keys to the chain which held his St. Christopher medal, and slipped it back over his head where it settled into the soft folds of his neck.

Glancing skyward, he made his way up the slope which would bring him to the path which was surrounded by the Zapote trees. Though the sky had cleared, a heavy mist lay low on the trail, its dampness making progress difficult. As he puffed and grew red-faced with the effort, he felt a strange heaviness in the air and heard mysterious rustling sounds. He looked around, saw nothing, and scoffed at himself, vowing to go on. Though the sense of foreboding raised his hackles, he trod onward, slipping here and there in the slick mud. The trail turned suddenly, sloping downward and catching him unaware. Before he could think, he was sloshing into an aguada, a shallow depression filled with water and weeds. Apprehension seized him, as he thought of snakes, scorpions and other nasty little jungle inhabitants. He struggled mightily and managed to slog out of the water and up the grass bank on the other side. Now he was covered with mud, wondering what other unwanted parasites had attached themselves to his clothes during his fall. Seeing that no one was on the deserted trail, he stripped himself of his shorts, boxers and clinging t-shirt, taking care not to dislodge the chain around his neck. Silently applauding his decision to leave his wallet safely locked in the car, he glanced ahead in naked splendor, looking for an answer to his dilemma.

Then, he heard the sound of water - running water. He walked toward the sound, carrying his wet, muddy clothes, and still wearing his sandals, which squished with each step. The sound grew stronger, and soon he was facing a steep waterfall, which flowed into an abandoned cenote. The cenote overflowed its banks, its waters coursing downstream, forming a series of shallow pools. He remembered the concierge at the hotel mentioning it, and knew it was not far from his destination. Meanwhile, it was a perfect place to clean his clothes, and himself. He leaned over the bank, and despite the scratchy grass, lay close to the edge and swirled his shorts and shirt in the clear cooling water, watching with satisfaction as the stream carried the dirt and leaves away, from pool to pool, taking all his worries and cares with them. He wrung the water out of them and laid them on the nearby rocks to dry. His sandals were still muddy and already wet, so he took them off and dunked them in and out, one in each hand, reveling in the cleansing ritual. But the ancient gods of the falls, watching this porcine human dabbling in their sacred water, became mischievous. Before Galindo could prevent it, his sunglasses slipped off his sweaty temples, joining in his ablutions with abandon. "Stop! No!" he yelled to the swirling waters beneath him. He rose suddenly, dropping his sandals into the mix, and catapulted off the bank attempting to grasp the glimmering gold rims of his aviators merrily bobbing their way down the stream on their way to the sea. Unfortunately for Galindo, as he entered the cenote, the resulting wave of water he created took with it yet another sacrifice to the capricious gods. The chain on which hung the rental car keys, accompanied by St. Christopher, swooshed over his head and sank to the depths of the old well, joining the sunken treasures from the necks of other victims. He thrashed about, trying to catch the sinking keys, but as he did, the current carried him downstream bumping over the barely submerged rocks which bruised his bare bottom. It was no small sacrifice on Galindo's part, but the gods were not yet assuaged.

Now in a state of panic, Galindo managed to halt his progress by burying his feet in a sandy shallow, and haul himself out by grasping the exposed roots of a shrub on the bank. As he finally plopped his bruised body out of the water, he heard rustling sounds again. He looked around, but saw no one. He thought the fruit picking crew may have heard his calls and were coming to his rescue. But not a soul appeared to assist him in his hour of desperation. Another rustle reached his ears, and he heard what sounded like a high pitched voice. He listened carefully again, but there was nothing but the caw of parrots and the buzz of a few dragonflies, lazily grazing the water. He tried to think reasonably, and decided that the best solution was to retrieve his clothes at the waterfall and retrace his steps down to the parking lot to see if he could somehow call for help at the tourist center which would no doubt be open by now. He would get hold of the manager's cousin and enlist him as a guide to the harvest spot. Barefoot and sunburned by now, as the morning sky had brightened, he carefully picked his way back through the grassy thicket, in the direction of the waterfall where he would find his clothes. He finally arrived, to receive yet another blow. There at the rock where he had left his clothes, was a flattened circle of grass, silvery green and serenely empty. He searched the area, squinting myopically through his unaided eyes, but there were no clothes anywhere. Was he at the wrong waterfall? The enormity of his predicament began to register. There he was in the middle of the jungle in the Yucatan, naked and frightened; no money, no keys, and no glasses. "Mi Dio!" He stepped on something in the grass, and feeling around, found his watch. Whoever or whatever took his clothes left in a hurry, leaving his watch behind. He picked it up, and holding it close to his eyes, read the time . . . 3:30. *"Ai, carrai!"* he wailed. By this time, he should have already seen to the loading of the fruit on the truck, and driven himself back to the Rey Caribe where he would be taking a nice cool shower, getting ready for the dance. Instead he was standing in a hot, steamy, god-forsaken jungle, sweating profusely and wearing nothing but a watch. And to make matters even worse, he could hear the sound of voices—voices speaking in a foreign tongue, drawing closer. And there around the bend were three Japanese tourists, walking his way and chattering happily. Could things possibly get any worse?

The gods of the sacred pool must have tired of their little game, and gifted Galindo with a good dose of clear-headed confidence. Suddenly emboldened, he pulled his considerable self together, drew himself up and took charge of the situation. He reached into the surrounding foliage with his hands, his eyes on the approaching tourists. He grabbed for the largest leaves he could find, and yanked them free from their stalks. Then, right hand front, left hand back, he covered his most prized parts with the giant greenery. Thus attired, he strode down the path, garbed like a sumo wrestler, nodding regally to the astonished threesome, and then to all he encountered before reaching the parking area. And there, amid the tour buses was his savior in the form of Jesus, the foreman of the workers he had hired. "Galindo!" Jesus shouted, waving frantically as he ran toward the strangely garbed figure of his boss.

Galindo, ecstatic upon seeing a familiar face, still grasping his covering, fought the impulse to hug Jesus, realizing at the last minute the result of dropping his hands from their leafy fans. Meanwhile, the sight of Galindo's state finally registered with Jesus. "Madre de Dios" he uttered. "You look terrible! What happened?" But before Galindo could explain, Jesus broke into laughter. "Galindo, mi amigo, I think I understand. Look behind you!" Before he turned, Galindo heard the same clatter of noise that had startled him at the cenote. He caught sight of the scene that had so amused Jesus. Two little lemurs, off their usual nocturnal schedules because of the eclipse, had roamed the jungle in the light of day, playfully stalking Galindo, and satisfying their curiosity by snatching the strange bundle he had left on the grass. They were natural mimics, and playfully adorned themselves with the garments, one wearing his t-shirt across his head, the other sporting his boxer shorts with the red hearts. They bounded, chattering as they ran, across the path behind

Galindo, and leapt up into the nearest tree, where they sat amongst the Zapotes, helping themselves to a juicy snack. "Carrai!" The trees were right here at the bottom of the path, probably all around him, but he failed to notice them in his haste to meet up with the men. He didn't have to go into the jungle at all.

Jesus covered Galindo with a blanket from his truck, and on the way home, relayed the story of the fatal accident that had befallen his friend, the pilot. When Galindo hadn't shown up, Jesus took it upon himself to get the harvested fruit loaded on the truck, and sent it to the airport via the ferry. After driving back to the hotel, his cousin, Jorge, told him of the plane crash, and that though it was rumored that Rudolfo had a passenger, there was no plane nor any survivors to be found. Jesus, knowing of the urgency to get the fruit back to Argentina, arranged for another cousin, twice removed, to employ a pilot friend of his to complete the mission. After hearing from Jorge that Galindo had rented the car early that morning, Jesus decided to return to the harvest area in case Galindo had gotten lost. Galindo blessed Jesus, and his many cousins and had thanked him many times by the time they pulled up to the hotel.

As he held the blanket around himself and stepped out of the truck, he was greeted by Miriam, who had been alerted by the hotel manager. She took one look at him, smiled and said, "Galindo, it's late! You look awful! Was there a problem?"

*　*　*

The tango workshop was alive with the news of the plane crash by the time we had returned from our shopping excursion. Gabriel and Graciela along with Claudio and Patricia were teaching their classes; Armando and Rosa, having reconciled, were holed up in Rosa's bungalow. Margo, not accustomed to venturing beyond her narrow bandwidth of caring, was going over her checklist for the evening's gala, and Efren was waiting for me in the little café where we were to meet for a late lunch. The buzz of the tragic accident finally found its way to the cafe. Efren took it in, momentarily gave the victims a prayer for their souls, and then brushed it off, as did the others. He was unaware of the impending surprise that Sara had planned; therefore oblivious to any connection between the news and any affect it might have on his world. I joined him, happy for his welcoming kiss, and we ate and talked and looked forward together to the events of the evening to come.

When I returned to our bungalow, the girls were resting, lying on their beds in their green clay masks like two refugee witches from the Land of Oz. Their eyes were covered with white cotton pads, soaked with another one of Dixie's "miracle potions." I had barely gotten my head on the pillow when the alarm rang. Dixie popped up, cleared her eyes of their coverings (I had to admit, they looked really good), and poked at Dawn. "Hey—get up!" she said. "The milonga starts in three hours—go ahead and shower and don't use all the hot water!" We couldn't wait to get into our purchases, and emptied them all on the bed. Dresses, shoes, jewelry, and lingerie tumbled out of the colorful bags, and we spent most of the next two hours trying them all on, then trying on each other's to make sure we liked our own, laughing and giggling like we were teenagers again. I think it was the best part of the weekend, except for Efren, of course. We had grown closer than ever before, and I had picked out the sexiest lingerie I could find, in secret anticipation of a lovely evening. I could imagine myself telling the girls not to worry if I didn't show up after the dance, laughing at their crude and sassy remarks as I would leave the ballroom on Efren's arm, maybe like Julia Roberts in "Pretty Woman."

The time finally came when no amount of primping would do any good, and the three of us headed up the hill to the ballroom like primadonnas. I was in blue like the color of the azure sea, Dixie in coral, and Dawn in pale lavender - her favorite. We all wore chiffon scarves in some form or other, which wafted in the gentle breeze. Dusk was giving way to twilight; the first star breaking through the dark blue canopy of the sky. It was an unusually large star, hanging just below the golden orb of the full moon. At the top of the hill, the entrance to the ballroom glowed with the lanterns that had been hung along the veranda, adding their golden glow to the burnished wood. The French doors were open so that we could hear the siren strains of the voluptuous tango music. We entered the transformed ballroom with delicious anticipation.

Dixie had her eye on a fellow named Patrick, whom she had met at a tango class back in the states. He hadn't impressed her much at the time, but in the classes, she had partnered him quite a bit, and he was really good! Besides, he had a twinkle in his eye, and quite the body. What's more, he couldn't keep his hands off her, to which she was happy to oblige. As she took off to find him, Dawn and I scanned the crowd. The scene before us delighted the senses. Swirls of light patterned the dance floor, catching the glitter of sequins of every imaginable hue. Couples were dancing by us with graceful intensity, creating a mélange of intoxicating scents in their wake. Tonight was definitely the women's night to shine and they looked spectacular. Casual culottes and tank tops worn in class gave way to sexy gowns, purchased weeks and maybe months before. The men looked dashing in their dark suits, playing the role that would give them the best advantage with the women; that of the handsome and intriguing tangueros they'd seen in the movies. A group of them stood in the corner, gossiping among themselves as avidly as women. What *were* they discussing? I wondered as I watched, and then decided it might be best that I didn't know. Luis came over and asked Dawn to dance, and I noticed Armando watching as she followed Luis to the floor. He was among the group of guys, fanning himself with a black lace fan. Rosa's, I supposed. Many of the men used fans, and didn't think a thing of it. I hoped Dawn was really over him, and started over to the buffet table when I felt a familiar arm around my waist. I looked up into Efren's eyes as he took me to the floor for a tango. They were gray and piercing, saying more than he could ever admit, or at least I thought so. We had just begun a molinete, when he suddenly stopped. I looked up at him, and he was staring over my head at the open French doors, his face ashen.

As I turned to look, the room hushed, and the music ceased. All eyes were on a beautiful woman being wheeled in by the imposing figure of an older gentleman. The woman had a cast on her leg, and her arm was in a sling. After what seemed like an eternity, someone shouted "Sara!" and then I realized that the sound was coming from

Efren. Simultaneously, the room became alive with voices, and though I could only catch a word here and there, I caught enough to know that the woman in the wheelchair was a passenger in the plane that crashed. Astounded and confused, I stood like a zombie as Efren rushed past me and knelt by her side, cradling her tenderly with the arms he had taken from around me.

Ah, the tango world. It reeks of drama! I was helpless in its power over me, and stood, transfixed as a distinguished gentleman made his way to the stage and took the microphone. "Ladies and gentlemen, *senoritas y senores;* allow me to introduce myself. I am Senor Adolfo Bautista, the producer of *El Tango Mejor.* This, as many of you know, is Sara Elizondo, the most beautiful and famous tango dancer from my show. I know you have questions, and rather than have it befall her to explain many times over, about her miraculous presence here, I think I can solve the mystery for you. Sara was coming here to surprise Efren. (Efren smiled as this was said) Unfortunately, the small plane she was traveling in, due to circumstances at the airport, crashed on the coastline of Bolivia, and fortunately landed in a large snowbank, which cushioning its landing, but covering it completely. Unfortunately, the pilot hit his head on impact, and did not survive. When Sara regained consciousness, she realized her predicament, and used a strip of metal from the instrument panel as a pole which she shoved above the snow like an antenna. The eclipse of the next morning delayed the search party, but when it ended, they sighted the antenna, flying a bright piece of intimate apparel. They found Sara huddled in blankets but amazingly alive, and took her to the hospital in Potosi. I was notified that afternoon, and went to her immediately. When I heard of her plight, and her desire to be with Efren, with the doctor's permission I brought her here to be reunited with her heart's desire. After all, isn't that what the tango tells us? It's all about love. And now, maestro, play your most beautiful tango for us, and let's dance".

The room erupted in applause. As I looked around, there were people laughing, crying, and hugging each other—even Margo. The room filled with the strains of a languid tango, and couples took to the floor with a new appreciation for each other. It was a touching scene, really, and I was happy that Sara's life had been spared. Yet, I envied her hold over Efren, and I regretted losing him. But, I really never had him, did I? Not all of him. I guess experience *is* what you get when you don't get what you want. Sighing, I headed up the stairs and retreated to the balcony.

*   *   *

Epilogue

The Resolution

Like putting the period at the end of a sentence, the time comes when the man will convey to the woman the impending dissolution of their three-minute tryst. It's all done cleanly and painlessly in three easy steps; one, two, three—back, side, together. Wham, bam, thank you, ma'am—and off he goes. Or, on occasion, he may draw his partner close, give her a lovely squeeze by way of thanks, and then, off he goes. I have decided that I am never ready for the tango to end.

So, that's my story—a good story with no moral, but a good lesson. There's truth in that saying: "The heart wants what the heart wants." Nothing more, nothing less. I always thought of myself as a mature woman who liked a safe harbor. I was in control of my life, and I tried to hold my desires in check, always prepared for the vagaries that fate might thrust upon me. But then this, after all, was the tango. Life longs for resolution, but with the tango, as in life, it never resolves. Like "El Molinete," it just keeps turning and turning, eventually turning in on itself. But then, doesn't all of life, really? We like to think it to be predictable and that we are in control, but when it comes down to it, we are at the center of a dynamic mélange of feelings and fantasies which we ourselves create in order to satisfy our longings. It's a crazy quilt we weave, whose patterns resemble the pixels in a primordial fern. I read about a scientist who conjectured that the paisley-like pattern that's found in every living cell is the thumbprint of God on his creation. God must be amused at how we've complicated the process of living life, and He must love us for trying so hard to make it all come out right.

As I climbed the narrow stairs to the balcony, I became more light-hearted, and chastised myself for taking everything so seriously. After all . . . the dance must eventually end as all good things do. The dancers will dance and love and cry, and dance again. The voyeur in me enjoyed the scene below, as I stood watching my friends and fellow students dance out their dramas. They rippled and swirled amongst the light and shadows like a school of tango fish—darting, gliding and skimming along in a vortex of color and emotion— willing sacrifices to the gods of the dance, baited by the music and their unfulfilled needs. How much will they be asked to give? All that they have. Is this any way to live? Oh, yes!

And then, a smiling face stood out, looking up at me from the crowd. It was Ricardo, giving me that almost imperceptible nod of his head—a silent command; "I've chosen you—come and dance with me." I smiled back, relinquishing my reverie for the moment. He was no Efren, but oh, could he dance! Down the stairs I went— and into his waiting arms.

*　　*　　*